ZERO

ZERO

ZERO

Diane Tullson

ZERO

Fitzhenry & Whiteside

Published in Canada by Fitzhenry & Whiteside, 195 Allstate Parkway, Markham, Ontario L3R 4T8

Published in the United States by Fitzhenry & Whiteside, 311 Washington Street, Brighton, Massachusetts 02135

www.fitzhenry.ca   godwit@fitzhenry.ca

Library and Archives Canada Cataloguing in Publication

Tullson, Diane, 1958–
    Zero / Diane Tullson.

ISBN-13: 978-1-55041-950-4
ISBN-10: 1-55041-950-1
    I. Title.
PS8589.U6055Z47 2006   jC813'.6   C2006-903244-0

U.S. Publisher Cataloging-in-Publication Data (Library of Congress Standards)

Tullson, Diane, 1958–
    Zero / Diane Tullson.
[192] p. : cm.
Summary: Kas has everything a teenager could possibly want. But Kas is hiding a secret—a secret so dangerous that it threatens to destroy not only her friendships, but also her own future.
ISBN-13: 978-1-55041-950-4 (pbk.)
ISBN-10: 1-55041-950-1 (pbk.)
1. Friendship — Juvenile fiction. I. Title.
[Fic] dc22   PZ7.T82318Ze 2006

Fitzhenry & Whiteside acknowledges with thanks the Canada Council for the Arts, and the Ontario Arts Council for their support of our publishing program. We acknowledge the financial support of the Government of Canada through the Book Publishing Industry Development Program (BPIDP) for our publishing activities.

 Canada Council   Conseil des Arts
for the Arts   du Canada

Design by Fortunato Design Inc.
Cover image by Tara Anderson

Printed in Canada

10 9 8 7 6 5 4 3 2

For S.H. and K.D.

JANUARY

Chapter One

"I'm fine, Dad. Really."

Kas adjusts the phone against her shoulder so that she can unpack while she talks. "My room is great."

She pulls the curtain back and looks out on to the front street. New snow covers the sidewalks and loads the spruce trees outside her window. Parked cars line one side of the road. One car inches its way past the others, its windshield wipers going full blast to clear the falling snow. Kas turns from the window.

"I even get my own TV, but I have to pay for the cable. I'll use the bank card you gave me."

Kas takes a photo of her family from her suitcase—her parents, two sisters, herself—all grinning. She sets the photo on the bedside table and aligns an alarm clock, a small sketchbook, and a pencil.

"The Greenes are nice. They took me on a tour of Whitchurch, showed me the highlights." She laughs.

"No, it didn't take long." She pauses. "They say I look just like their daughter when she was sixteen." Kas surveys her reflection in the mirror over the dresser. She turns to one side, then the other, then strains over her shoulder to see her butt. The mirror is too high, and she has to jump to see.

"The other tenant? No, it's a guy. I haven't met him yet, but he keeps his bathroom cabinet very tidy." A can of shaving cream, an inexpensive razor, toothpaste with the lid on, floss—she had sipped a tiny swig of his mouthwash. It had burned the back of her throat.

"Mrs. Greene says he's a year ahead of me, in grade twelve." Kas pulls open her dresser and rearranges her socks in the drawer.

"He studies music, I think. He has a keyboard in his room." She closes the drawer.

"Listen, Dad, it's just about time for supper. I'll call you tomorrow, okay?" She zips the suitcase closed and slides it under her bed.

"Dad, I'm fine. Tomorrow I'll tell you all about the school. Say hi to Mom. Love you too." She snaps the phone closed and tosses it on the bed.

In the mirror, Kas adjusts her reddish-brown hair over her shoulders, tries it behind her ears, then gathers it into a quick knot. Her reflected eyes watch her from the mirror. She finishes with her hair, reaches for her makeup kit, and grabs a lipstick. Her mother says it's too dark for her pale skin. Downstairs, Mrs. Greene is calling her to dinner. Kas tugs the elastic out of her hair. With one last glance in the mirror, she sighs and heads downstairs.

She's early. Kas stands on the sidewalk in front of the school—Whitchurch Secondary School of the Arts, a three-story brick building. On the front steps, a custodian sweeps away the snow, his breath puffing out in clouds. Kas grips her art portfolio with both gloved hands. Winter air creeps under her coat, and she shivers. Whitchurch is only a few hours drive to the north from home, but this morning it feels arctic-cold.

Too early. Maybe she could walk back up to Main, grab a coffee. The sidewalk has been cleared by one of those big sweeper trucks, and Kas sees hard-packed footprints from someone who had walked up to the school before it was swept. With the toe of her shoe she dislodges one of the footprints and kicks it off the sidewalk.

"You here to see Dr. Dee?"

Kas jumps, then laughs. The custodian is leaning on his broom, watching her. She says to the custodian, "I'm here to see the principal, Dr. D'Angelo."

"That's Dr. Dee. She's here." The custodian motions to the front door. "It's open."

Kas thanks him and pushes open the front door, grateful for the rush of warm air. She pulls off her gloves and jams them in her pockets. To her left, she sees the door marked Office. To her right, a large chrome sculpture gleams under a skylight. She stamps a bit of snow from her shoes, and the sound echoes in the hall. Kas steps over to the sculpture.

Polished metal tubes catch her reflection again and again, wrapping her like ribbons onto the wrought spirals.

The effect disorients her, and Kas sets her hand on the sculpture to steady herself. Under her hand, the sculpture begins to move. Kas grabs at it, afraid it's going to fall, and the thing turns, picking up speed until her reflection swirls up the metal tubes. Kas puts her hands over her eyes.

"It's called Vortex."

Kas drops her hands. A guy is at the office door, a student—sweatshirt, jeans, gold-brown hair hanging nicely just to his eyes. He's walking toward her.

"You didn't break it. It's meant to move." He gives the sculpture another spin. "You set it in motion, then it builds its own momentum." His reflection and hers spin together in the spiraling sculpture. Kas has to turn her head away.

He says, "You must be the new student." He motions to her portfolio. "Visual Arts, right? You're staying with the Greenes."

Her eyes widen and she says, "This really *is* a small town."

He laughs. "I board there too. I knew someone had moved in—figured it was probably you."

The taste of his mouthwash seems suddenly very strong. She resists an urge to step back from him. She says, "I haven't seen you at the house."

He nods. "Weird schedule right now, at work."

The office door swings open, and a woman steps into the hall. She's tall, her red hair short and wild, and she's wearing jeans and a long-sleeved T-shirt. On her feet she sports bright yellow sneakers.

"Kas?" She strides over, extends her hand. "Welcome. You've met Jacob, I see."

"Jacob." She glances at him, and he smiles. Nice smile. He says, "Glad you're here, Kas."

The principal introduces herself, then ushers Kas toward the office. "You're going to love Whitchurch. Students are great. It helps that everyone wants to be here." She laughs. "You've missed a couple of weeks in this term, but you'll get caught up."

Kas looks back at Jacob. Nice eyes, gray and green at the same time.

Nice guy. Very nice.

Chapter Two

Kas grabs a cafeteria tray and loads it with yogurt and an apple. She orders a bowl of vegetable soup. The worker behind the steam table hums to himself as he ladles her soup. The label on his apron says he's a student volunteer. Kas jams her chin farther into her turtleneck.

"Want some crackers?" The guy motions to a basket of saltines on the stainless steel counter. "Special deal, just for you." He snags two packets and tucks them beside her soup bowl.

"You know a good customer when you see one." Kas feels the nudge of the line behind her. "Thanks."

She turns to maneuver her tray toward the cashier and feels it again. Someone behind her in the line is bumping her. She turns. Jacob, grinning, is standing with a laden tray.

"You sitting with someone?"

Before she can answer him, a girl tips her head around Jacob. "Hey, it's Kas, right?"

Kas smiles at her. "Yes. Wellness class, yesterday—right?"

The girl grins. "Glorified gym class, you mean. Only at an arts school would P.E. be called Wellness."

The girl is perfectly made up and wears a snug white sweater and tiny jeans. The guy with the soup ladle has stopped to gaze at the girl, his ladle suspended over a soup bowl, his face registering adoration. The girl glances at him.

He finds his voice, then stutters, "Hey, M-Marin."

"Hey, Bal." She turns back to Kas, and in the smallest of motions, rolls her eyes. Jacob says, "So, are you sitting with anyone?"

Kas feels herself beginning to blush.

Marin waves her hand. "What do you think? She just got here. I remember what that's like." She sidles past Jacob and moves her tray to the cashier. The tray has nothing on it but a can of Diet Pepsi. She says, "Sit with us."

Kas pays, then follows dumbly as Marin leads her through a sea of crowded tables. Marin, her long black hair swaying, slides into a table already packed with people, then shoves down the bench to make room for Kas and Jacob. Kas hesitates a moment, waiting for Jacob to sit down next to Marin, but he motions for her to take the spot.

Marin pops open her Diet Pepsi, smiles, and says, "Welcome to Whitchurch: school for the self-absorbed and the self-obsessed."

Kas peels the lid off her carton of yogurt. She skims her spoon over the top of the yogurt, then licks the spoon. "I should resent that. Except that you're probably right."

She sets down her spoon and says to Marin, "No paint on your clothes; no clay in your hair. You must be in Performing Arts."

Marin nods. "Acting. I know you're an artist. Jacob told me."

She glances at Jacob, who is plowing through a sandwich. He swallows, then says, "You have good music."

He must have heard it this morning even though she played it low—or in the middle of the night. She makes a mental note to get headphones.

She asks Marin, "Where are you boarding?"

Marin sips the soda, then touches the tip of her tongue to her top lip. "Oh, my mother wouldn't let me live away from home. When I got accepted at Whitchurch, she moved us here. My dad commutes three hours a day to the city. But, hey, we're all together."

Kas thinks briefly of her mother, of her face when the letter arrived from Whitchurch after Christmas, finally announcing that Kas could join for the second semester. Conflicted. That's how her mother looked.

Marin says, "A word of warning." She gestures to Kas's soup. "I wouldn't eat anything they make here. Every recipe starts with a pail of lard."

Kas studies her soup. Marin sets a manicured fingernail on the rim of the bowl. "See it? All those globules?"

Kas pushes the soup away. "Different school, same food."

Marin glances at Jacob, bent over his lunch tray. "They're killing us with it." She swings her legs over the bench. "Come on, Kas. Let's just get something from the machines."

"Uh, oh. My mother is home." Marin points to the Volvo in the driveway. "I thought she was working today."

Kas burrows deeper into her coat. "I can get your math notes another time."

"No." Marin sighs. "We may as well get this over with. My apologies in advance."

Marin opens the front door. Immediately Kas can hear the sound of heels on the stone floor. Marin's mother clicks into the entryway—her belted slacks sharply creased, her blouse collar turned up with precision. Marin's mother welcomes Kas and takes Marin's backpack from her. "I'm Joy Jennett. It's nice to meet you."

Marin takes Kas's pack and jacket, and tosses them on a chair. She slides open the closet door and slings her jacket on a hook. She traces her fingers over the stenciled lettering of a nameplate above the hook. To Kas she quietly says, "M-A-R-I-N. That's me. Just in case I get confused. Aren't the tulips a nice touch?" She slides the closet door closed with a thump.

"You both probably need a snack. Come into the kitchen and I'll make you a fresh sandwich. I bought some nice cheese today, and tomatoes—"

Marin cuts her off. "In a little while. Okay, Mom? We just want to relax right now."

Marin's mother stands a little straighter and says, "How about a glass of milk? You must be thirsty, at least."

"Well, Mother, there are fountains at school."

"I'm aware of that, Marin, as well as there being pop machines and vending machines on every floor—all filled with junk food. You can't look your best at an audition if you're filling up on junk."

Marin sighs. "No chips, no chocolate. I swear. Do you want a urine test?"

"It's for your own good. You know how sensitive your skin is." She directs her attention to Kas. "Maybe Kas would like something?" She pronounces it so it rhymes with ass. She looks Kas up and down.

Kas opens her mouth to speak but Marin cuts her off. "It's *Kazz*. And she had a huge lunch. We'll be in my room if you need me."

"Audition?"

Marin flops down on the bed and throws one arm across her face. "Our end of term production is *Macbeth*. My mom wants me to play Lady Macbeth. She says I should get the role because I model and act."

Kas sits on the chair by Marin's desk. "Are you famous?"

Marin laughs. "I did a TV spot for Hasbro. Mostly I model."

"I've never met a real model before."

Marin rolls over on to her side to face Kas. "Mom thinks it will help my acting career. I don't talk about it much because it makes some people uncomfortable."

"Like, jealous, you mean?"

"Just some people."

Kas says, "Art students take turns modeling, at least we did at my old school."

"Nude?"

"Don't scare me. I've never had to model, though. I erased my name on the list."

"And no one noticed?"

"If they did, I doubt they'd object."

"You have fabulous hair. When the light hits it, it looks as if it's on fire."

"You should see it in the morning. It looks like someone put out a fire in it."

Marin shudders. "Mornings should be canceled."

Kas says, "Sometimes I sleep in my makeup so I don't have to face myself in the morning."

"Ooh, my mother would have a small fit about that. Talk about clogging your pores."

"Think of the time I save in the morning."

"Especially if you dressed the night before."

"And had breakfast the night before."

"Or not." Marin pauses. "If I looked like you, I could face myself in the morning."

Kas guffaws, "Yeah, right."

"Jacob seems to like what he sees."

Kas stutters a bit when she says, "So, you and Jacob aren't going out?"

"I adore Jacob." Marin waves her hand. "We're just friends, though. We're all friends here. Everyone knows everyone. And everything about everyone. The school isn't big enough for secrets, and the town…" Marin pauses, shakes her head. "The town is way too small."

Alone in her room Kas sits at her desk, a sketchbook open in front of her. Through the window, in the bell of the streetlight, she watches snow falling. Downstairs she hears the sound of dishes being cleared. Jacob isn't there. They said he was working, that he cleans at the municipal animal shelter. Mrs. Greene made a plate for him and put it in the oven.

Kas gets up from the desk and counts the steps to the door. Out in the hall, Jacob's door stands open, his room dark. Beyond Jacob's room, at the end of the hall, the bathroom door stands ajar. On tiptoe, Kas counts the steps to Jacob's door.

Chapter Three

The doctor's office in Whitchurch is in an old house on Millard Road. The waiting room is the former front parlor. A dentist shares the space; Kas can smell drilled teeth. An ancient woman in a white smock sits behind a desk. She hands Kas a clipboard.

Smiling, the woman says, "Please fill in the patient information. The doctor will see you shortly."

Kas wonders why she has to fill out this form. Surely her doctor at home forwarded her records. She's not sure even why new students need this, but Dr. D'Angelo was adamant. Mandatory. No exceptions. Must be done.

Kas takes a seat and scans the form—Name, Address, Health Plan. These she fills in. Gender. Age. Then a long list of questions about family history, diabetes, heart disease, high blood pressure. Barely reading them, Kas ticks the *No* box to each question. If it makes Dr. Dee happy, then she'll do it. Anything, so she can go to Whitchurch. Graduating from Whitchurch practically assures entrance into the best art colleges, and why would she want to study anywhere else?

The woman calls her name, and Kas follows her up a creaking staircase—the woman wheezing softly—to a small room at the top of the stairs. The paper on the examination table is creased from a previous patient. It is stained with a tiny smear of blood. Kas feels her breath catching in her chest and thinks it better not be a full physical. The woman peels back the paper from the examination table and wads it into a huge ball, then she unrolls fresh paper over the table. She motions to a scale in the corner of the room.

"Let's get your weight, dear."

Kas swallows. "Fully dressed?"

The woman is penciling Kas's name onto the chart, her handwriting spidery and pale. Kas isn't sure if she heard her. As quickly as she can, Kas drops her coat into a chair, kicks off her boots, and steps on the scale. The woman peers down to read the needle on the scale, then enters the figure onto the chart.

"The doctor will be right in." She closes the door, and Kas hears the stairs creaking as she goes down.

She hears a low rumble of voices from the next room. Another patient and the doctor, she guesses. Oh good. Walls like paper. Kas opens the cupboard over the sink. Jars of swabs. Tongue depressors. The door opens and she jumps back.

The doctor is clearly a match for the old woman downstairs. His snow-white hair is parted exactly down the side; his white eyebrows curl luxuriantly over his pale blue eyes, and lines ridge his face. He nods at Kas and extends his hand. "I'm Dr. Bowen." He pronounces it *bone*. His hand feels leathery and dry. "And you must be Kasandra."

"Kas, actually."

He makes a note on the chart. His handwriting reveals a small shake. "Kas." He settles onto a black leather stool. "Sit down, Kas." He gestures with his pen to the paper-covered table. She perches on the edge of the table, aware of the paper crinkling beneath her. The doctor pulls a large brown envelope from her folder. Kas recognizes the return address as the clinic at home. He skims the letter, then flips through the papers. Then he glances at her. "Well, you look healthy enough."

The doctor pushes himself to his feet and wraps a blood pressure belt around her arm. He slips the stethoscope under the edge of the band and studies her with pale blue eyes as he listens to her heartbeat. His upper lip is pleated with wrinkles, and a missed swath of whiskers bristles on his cheek. He has a spot of lunch on the front of his smock. Finally he releases the blood pressure band.

"Normal."

She breathes.

The doctor listens to her chest, checks her reflexes. He folds his stethoscope into his pocket. "Enjoying the school?"

"It's great."

"Homesick?"

She shrugs. She does miss her parents. And her younger sisters—well, no, she doesn't miss them much. They're probably glad they don't have to deal with her moods, her *issues*.

She says, "Sometimes."

The doctor closes Kas's folder. "You'll be busy at that school. That'll help."

He opens the door to the hallway. "Very nice meeting you." And he's gone.

Chapter Four

Kas and Marin lean in to the washroom mirror, dabbing pearls of makeup over their eyes. Kas says, "If they found out makeup causes cancer, would you stop wearing it?"

Marin laughs.

"I'm serious. If everyone went without makeup, then our real faces would be, you know, real."

"Real scary," Marin says. "Real is what people see, so real *is* makeup. No question."

"Is a nose job real, or a boob job?"

"What's your point?"

"Say you get a nose job."

Marin examines hers in the mirror.

"You get a nose job and turn it into a perky little upturn. Then you meet a guy and get married. As far as he knows, you were born with that nose."

"I'd get mine done in a heartbeat." Marin pushes the end of her nose from side to side. "Unless you told him, he'd never know. There are no scars. They do all the work from up your nostrils."

Kas leans against the sink, watching Marin. "So, what if your baby inherits your real nose—which is fine, by the way—isn't that some kind of betrayal to the father?"

"I say, 'Buyer, beware.' Guys get them done too." Marin tosses her makeup bag into her purse. "What are you saying? That we should go around without makeup, reveal all our flaws? Why not just strip us all naked, cut to the awful truth?"

Kas studies her reflection in the mirror. "I wouldn't be caught dead naked. All I'm saying is that no one really knows anything about other people. It's makeup, or clothes, or some other disguise. No one reveals anything." Kas strains over her shoulder to see her butt.

"And everyone is happier that way." Marin turns and looks at her backside in the mirror as well. "Do these jeans make my butt look fat?"

"Size zero jeans cannot make your butt look fat."

"Size zero—in my dreams." She nudges up against Kas and hip checks her. "Those jeans look great on you. They make your butt look smaller."

"Oh, thanks," Kas says. "I think."

Kas finds Marin at their usual lunchtime meeting place: the pop machines. Kas drops her coins into the machine and collects her Diet Pepsi. Marin takes her arm. "Come on. I'll show you the bomb shelter."

Kas follows Marin down two flights to the basement of the school, then down one more flight to the auxiliary gym weight room.

"This used to be the main weight room for the school before the new one was built on the gym level," Marin says. "It's more of a storeroom now." The space is windowless, lined with a maze of storage boxes, set props, and general school debris. In the center of the room, a four-station weight machine clanks as a couple of guys work out. Kas and Marin make their way past them. They greet Marin, give Kas a quick once-over, then return to their exercise. Marin pulls open a heavy door to reveal the tunnel.

"I always prop the door open." She uses a large-sized water bottle, almost full. "The door isn't locked, but just in case…"

The tunnel is an immense, cinder-block snake: walls painted white, white tile floor, caged bulbs on the ceiling. Kas rubs her arms. "I've never been in a bomb shelter before." She looks up at the lights. "These are always on?"

Marin settles on the floor. "Apparently. I guess they figure that if the Big One drops, they won't have time to find a light switch."

Kas sinks down against the wall beside Marin. "The bulbs never burn out?"

Marin lights a cigarette and speaks through the smoke. "The district hires the Whitchurch junior hockey team to come down here a couple times a year. They patch any cracks, change the bulbs, paint out graffiti. That's how I know about the tunnel. Junior hockey." She smiles.

Kas waves away the smoke. "Doesn't smoking dull

your complexion, not to mention what it does to your lungs?"

"It doesn't cause zits, so it qualifies as tolerable self-abuse." She exhales, her eyes narrowing against the smoke. "My mother smokes in her bathroom. Apparently she quit years ago."

"So, why does no one else come down here?"

Marin looks up at the bare lights. "It's not the most comfortable place." She inhales, then lifts her chin and exhales toward the ceiling. "I like it because it's the only place inside the school without smoke detectors."

"Where does this tunnel lead?"

"Nowhere. A brick wall. I guess it used to connect to something."

Kas pops open her Diet Pepsi and takes a sip. "Narnia, maybe."

Marin finishes her cigarette, breathing the smoke, exhaling impatiently. She butts it on the floor. "Scary thought—the entire school crammed down here. Can you imagine the stink? I'd take my chances with the Bomb."

Kas pulls the sleeves of her sweater down over her hands. "Ever wonder what it would be like to get stuck down here?"

"The door doesn't lock."

"I know. But if it got jammed or something." Kas pauses. "I guess someone would hear us banging on the door."

Marin grins. "Yeah, but it could take a while. What if we starved?"

Kas pauses, then says, "You think anyone has ever died down here?"

Marin sniffs the air and says, "Only smells like it." Marin lights another cigarette, and Kas watches her hands, white skin stretched over fine bones. Marin holds the cigarette with fingers so straight that Kas wonders if she learned to smoke from watching old movies. Kas says, "If I were drawing your hands, I'd draw a bird. Or a tree branch, from a sapling tree."

Marin raises her eyebrows.

"The smallest branch of a willow tree—I'd use charcoal to mark the whiteness of the bark."

Marin turns her hand, palm up. "And the lines could be veins on leaves."

"Yes!"

Marin laughs. "Maybe I should be a hand model. Then I wouldn't have to worry about zits."

Kas peels a Band-Aid from her finger and reveals a crescent-shaped cut marked with red.

"Have you ever seen an art injury before?"

"Why would I want to?" But Marin examines the wound. Her hair falls across her face—black hair, white skin. She wrinkles her nose. "Gross."

Kas presses on the finger, and the line bulges with blood. She says, "The teacher, Mr. Randall, said he had a student once who put the blade right through the end of his finger and stuck it in the table. The teacher had to pull it out."

Marin drops her hand. "If I saw that, I would throw up." She tips her head back against the concrete wall and closes her eyes.

Chapter Five

Kas stands still at Jacob's door, watching him. His back is to her as he sits at his keyboard. He has headphones on, so it makes no sound when he presses the keys. His shoulders move in small waves with the music, and Kas imagines she can hear it. From time to time, he pauses and writes in a composition book. His arms, bent over the keys, are long for his T-shirt—strong, lean arms. Long fingers, graceful, pulling the music from the keys. A lamp on his desk shines behind him so that around his face his hair gleams golden. She imagines that he closes his eyes as he plays. She closes hers.

"Hey, Kas."

He's looking at her as she stands there in his doorway, in her robe and fuzzy socks, with her mouth gaping. She feels her cheeks turn crimson.

He laughs, takes off the headphones. "I didn't hear you. Sorry. Come on in."

Kas shakes her head. "No, I'm sorry. I didn't mean to disturb you."

He flicks a towel off the end of the bed. "Come on. I'll play it for you."

She perches on the edge of the bed. His room is like

hers: the bed and furniture the same, the same desk by the window. His window blinds are down but the slats are turned so that the streetlight pools on his desk.

"It's classical, so don't go running away."

"I like classical music." That's not quite true.

As if he knows that, he says, "Uh huh. It's for my composition course. Sometimes I think they let me in to Whitchurch just so they'd have someone to operate the sound boards."

"Play it."

He smiles, turns to the keyboard, and adjusts the volume. "I don't want to wake up the Greenes."

Then he starts to play. Kas wraps her hands around her knees. The sound is at first complex, but when she closes her eyes, she can hear the strands of his composition, how he's woven the notes to create new sound. He finishes, and when she opens her eyes, he's watching her.

She says, "I already knew I liked it."

"Then it's yours. When it's done, that is."

Kas gets up. "I should go."

He hangs his headphones on a hook by the keyboard. "I'm glad you liked it."

She stands a moment more. "Sometimes when I draw, I imagine the lines are words, as if the drawing is whispering a story to me."

He nods. "I'd like to hear that story."

As she falls asleep, she can still hear his music.

Chapter Six

Kas tugs her headband lower over her ears, focusing on long strides as she runs. If she were at home, she'd be with her mother and sisters at the breakfast table right now. Her dad would be leaving for work. He'd kiss her, and she'd smell peanut butter and coffee, the smells arriving in layers. The Greenes have left for work. Jacob is still sleeping.

She pumps her arms, not so hard that people notice but hard enough that she's starting to feel a familiar ache in the front of her shoulders. *Run.* It's still dark, but there's enough light on the streets; and anyway, it's not as if anyone is going to attack her. *Run.* She draws the pre-dawn air into her lungs, exhaling hard to drive it out. Where the sidewalks haven't been cleared, her feet crunch in the snow. She turns and looks at her footprints, soft craters in the snow, the waffle tread of her running shoes clearly defined. Ahead of her, the lights of town dwindle to the darkness of farm fields and forests.

Run.

Kas rips the page from her sketchbook and hurls it into the trash can. Next to her, another student, Stephanie,

27

glances up from her work. She says, "Kas, that was good!"

Kas wraps her arms around herself. "It was garbage."

Stephanie holds her own sketchbook at arm's length and examines it. "I know garbage, and that was not garbage."

Kas looks over at the girl's page. It is a sketch of the bowl of fruit that Mr. Randall had arranged on the front table. Kas says, "Wow. You really get this assignment."

Stephanie's eyebrows lift, questioning.

"No, I mean it. Your drawing is amazing."

She smiles. "When I applied to Whitchurch, there were four other people from my school trying to get in, all of them amazing artists. I got in; they didn't. But once I arrived here, it didn't mean anything." She gestures to work tacked up around the room. "Here at Whitchurch, I'm average."

Kas follows her gaze around the room. "I know. At my old school, they selected my work for the yearbook and commencement folders." She looks down at the stark white page of her sketchbook. "Everything I do here feels juvenile."

"I love your style. It's raw."

Kas rocks back and forth on the chair. "Rotten, maybe, like the fruit."

"You are talented, Kas. Everyone can see that."

Kas smiles at her.

Stephanie says, "You better give Mr. Randall at least a

sketch today. He's absolutely anal about deadlines."

Kas slouches back in her chair.

Rotten, rotten, rotten.

She grabs a stick of charcoal and makes a quick sketch. "I hope he likes black bananas."

hey mom and dad:

i just wanted to thank you for letting me come to Whitchurch. i can't describe how it is making me grow as a person. i feel so grounded here, so connected to the creative forces. i'm so happy. the teachers are amazing. my drawing teacher, mr. randall, he is so emotionally nurturing. it's as if he's a father, and no, he's not a pervert. not that you'd think that. ha ha. i'm doing my best work here and it's so exciting. i feel like i'm alive and i'm so healthy, so strong. i'm happy. really, really happy. so thanks. i love you both. please hug the sisters for me. and punch them too. just jokes.

love,

kas

Chapter Seven

"Black bananas?" Mr. Randall stands back from her charcoal drawing. "An unusual take on the classic bowl of fruit."

Half of the class is huddled near the music player arguing over what disc to play. Others wear headphones and listen to their own tunes as they work at their stations. Kas cleans her fingers on a scrap of towel.

"You've never let a banana go black?"

"Not so many as you've drawn. I can't see a bowl, or background, or anything except black lines."

She concentrates on the tabletop in front of her. Tiny scratches mar the surface. They make her think of an ice rink, and she wishes she had a Zamboni to polish it perfectly clean. She says, "Black bananas are actually better for you. The sugars are more developed."

"My wife uses black bananas for some loaf she makes."

"That would be banana loaf?"

He moves aside and flips through her portfolio. "I'd like to see one of your sketches for the still-life project."

She glances up at him. "You're looking at it."

He taps the paper on her table. "Not this. I want to see the still life I assigned: apples, oranges, bananas, in a bowl, on a table cloth, on a table."

Maybe the Zamboni could erase Mr. Randall too. "I thought you might like a still life with some originality."

"I would. Why don't you do one for me?"

"I thought I had."

He leans closer to the blackened paper on her table and speaks quietly. "Your work is good, Kas. Really good. The still-life drawing is a major portion of the term's grade. The Latcham Gallery downtown displays Whitchurch work. Students have sold pieces there, Kas. I'd like to put your work in the gallery, but if this sketch is any indication of the finished drawing, I couldn't."

He studies the paper. "This is so far from what you can achieve that I'd fail it on those grounds alone."

She sits back in her chair. "You'd fail this?"

Don't cry. Do not cry.

"It's completely without composition. It looks as if you've covered the paper with charcoal; as if you want to disguise it; as if you covered up some work you weren't happy with."

Tiny scratches on her table, but if you could look down into them, they would take you deep, beyond light.

"Someone with your talent could easily draw a passing-grade still life. You could do it with your eyes closed."

She takes the paper from the table and folds it.

"I'll re-do it." She folds the paper again, and once more. Beside her, Stephanie turns and looks, then quickly looks away. Black charcoal powders Kas's hands. Mr. Randall pulls a chair up next to Kas. "You can draw life, Kas. Find the life, in the sunlight on the table, in the flesh of the fruit, in the earth of the bowl. Use charcoal if you want, but use it to define the life, not shadow it."

He gets up from the chair. "Give yourself enough time to finish this project. If it's late, I'll have to penalize you."

"I won't be late."

"Fine." He pauses, then says, "The best artists know how to take criticism."

"Right."

Stephanie reaches across the washroom sink and hands Kas a length of paper towel. "It's Mr. Randall's favorite project. He makes all his classes do it."

"I hate still life. Why not call it still death? Where's the life in a stupid bowl of fruit?" Kas swipes at the tears now spilling from her eyes. "He said I'd fail. If I fail, they send me home. If I get sent home, I can't get into college." She jabs at the mascara running under her eyes.

Stephanie puts her hand on Kas's arm. "Whoa. You're not going to fail. Just give him what he's asking for. You can do it, Kas." She squeezes Kas's arm. "Your work is perfect. He's coming down hard on you because he knows you can deliver."

"Pizza."

Stephanie laughs. And she can't help it; Kas laughs too. She says, "I'm sorry to dump on you."

Stephanie pulls her into a hug. "If you knew Whitchurch was going to be this hard, would you still have applied?"

Kas sighs. "Yes."

"Me too."

Kas sits up, then reaches for a dumbbell by the bed. She curls the dumbbell up and down, watching her bicep swell and release. Up. Down. Sweat begins to bead on her forehead. She has to be quiet; she doesn't want to wake Jacob. He's sleeping. She knows this without seeing him because his door is closed, but she imagines that she can hear him breathing—that if she crept to his door and listened, she could hear him breathing in his sleep. Her bicep is aflame.

Breathe. The burn is a good thing. Breathe. Burn. Breathe. Burn.

FEBRUARY

Chapter Eight

There's a tap on the bathroom door. Kas jumps, snaps off the water. She hears Jacob's voice. "What are you doing in there?"

She didn't know he was home. She checks her face in the mirror, her hair. She glances around the bathroom, drops her toothbrush back into its holder. She opens the door.

Jacob stands in his blue work uniform, the shirt tucked into his pants. Kas lingers on the lean line of his body. She says, "Sorry. Was I taking too long?"

"I thought you might be getting washed down the drain."

His eyes look gray tonight. "I'm a little obsessed when I brush my teeth."

"I'm surprised there's anything left of them."

Gray eyes, with flecks of green that make her think of unfurled leaves—more a promise of green than the actual color. "It's all yours." She moves out of the bathroom, motioning with a flourish for him to enter.

"That's okay. I just wanted to make sure you were all right."

"Perfectly fine. This bathroom is one hundred percent accident-free."

"Once, my sister shaved with a dull razor. She ripped strips of flesh off both ankles. The bathroom looked like a crime scene."

Kas glances again around the bathroom. Nothing out of place. "I guess I know how to shave my legs."

He blushes bright red. "I didn't mean—"

She laughs. "I know. Your sister—is she younger?"

"Older. This was a few years ago." The red creeps out of his face. "She's at university now."

"Art school?"

He shakes his head. "Engineering. Everyone in my family goes into Engineering."

"So you're the black sheep."

"I prefer to think of myself as a renegade."

"Renegade. I like that."

He watches her for a moment, then smiles. "You have nice teeth."

She grins to show her teeth. "Braces—two years—and a rather nasty dental appliance that came with a key."

"That was a good disc you were playing this morning."

She thinks back. "Live Aid. They should have let U2 keep playing." His hair curls on the collar of his shirt. She says, "So, you were at work?"

Duh.

"Uh huh."

"Whitchurch has an animal shelter? It barely has a motel."

"We get a lot of animals. People from the city dump their pets out on the highway when they're done with them. They end up in town, eating out of the trash cans."

"And these animals get adopted?"

He pauses a moment, then says, "Mostly. What was for supper?"

"Mrs. Greene saved you a plate. It was some kind of pasta with eggplant." She grimaces.

"Sounds good." He sticks his hands in his pocket, drops his chin. He says, "So I guess you've eaten already."

She should do some more homework, maybe a workout. His eyelashes practically touch his cheekbones. She says, "More or less."

He shifts from foot to foot. "You want some tea or something? I'll put on the kettle for you."

She can work out later. "I'll come down with you."

He grins.

The house is dark. Kas hears the Greenes' TV in their room, and a light shines under their door. She flips on the light over the sink. At the table, Mrs. Greene has left a place set for Jacob. He opens the oven, and with the dishtowel, brings out a foil-covered plate. The smell of cheese and noodles makes Kas's mouth water.

She says, "The blackish bits are eggplant. I'd try to avoid those."

He pulls up his chair and dives into the mountain of pasta. He eats with such ease, like he's not even thinking about it. Halfway through his plate he looks up. "Sorry, I should have offered you some."

She puts up her hand. "No, really. I'm fine."

He resumes his attack on the pasta. She says, "Want some milk?"

He nods, swallows his mouthful, and says, "Yes, please."

She grabs two glasses and a carton of skim. She fills his glass. He takes the milk and gulps it down. He gets up, brings a loaf of bread from the counter. With a piece of bread, he mops up the last of his dinner. Then he takes another piece of bread and butters it. From a shelf by the table, he gets a jar of peanut butter and slathers on a thick layer. She laughs; she can't help it.

He pauses with his hand in midair, holding the half-eaten peanut butter sandwich. "What?"

"I can't believe you're so thin."

He shrugs. "Gotta eat." He finishes the bread. "Now for dessert." He pops a slice of bread into the toaster, then gets up for a jar of cinnamon from Mrs. Greene's spice rack. He says, "Brown sugar or white?"

"Brown?"

He returns to the table with a container of brown sugar. He opens it, and they both lean over to inhale.

"Brown. Definitely," he says. The toast pops up, and he butters it, then sprinkles it with cinnamon and a generous coating of sugar. He cuts it and pushes half toward her.

She takes a small bite. The sugar crunches against her teeth, and her entire mouth responds. The cinnamon she receives high on her palate, tasting it as much with her nose as her mouth. She takes another bite, then a bigger bite. She tongues her teeth, gathering any remnants of sweetness.

Jacob is smiling at her. "Want another one?"

She watches mutely as he makes two slices. She takes the toast from him, tears off a tiny corner, trying to eat it politely.

"I beat you," he says, wiping crumbs from his mouth.

There's a glisten of butter on his lips. He puts two more slices into the toaster. She laughs. They're down to the last of the loaf, and they arm wrestle for the heel, their elbows crunching crumbs on the table, their hands slippery with grease. She can smell him: his shampoo, his shirt, even his underarms—but it's a nice smell. He wins the arm wrestle, of course. But he gives her the last piece of toast.

Chapter Nine

"You didn't!"

In the school washroom, Marin sits on the counter by the sinks. Marin says, "I never eat anything after six at night."

"It was just two pieces of toast." Or three. Or four. "And you're missing the point about Jacob. I had such a good time with him. It's like I can be totally myself with him."

Marin doesn't seem to hear. "You can't hope to burn off calories before you go to bed, and it turns into lard over night."

Kas swallows. In the mirror, she examines her hips. "You can't see it, can you?"

Marin tosses up her hands. "The damage is done, Kas. All you can do is make up for it."

"What do you mean?"

"Don't eat, of course. What else?" She jumps down from the counter and gathers Kas into a hug. "Don't beat yourself up about it. Everyone slips." She turns Kas so they're facing the mirror. "You're gorgeous. Say it."

"You're gorgeous."

"Ha, ha. *You're* gorgeous, Kas. Come on, say it."

"It."

"Okay, fine. But you are."

Kas says, "When I was younger, my thighs didn't touch."

"Really?"

Kas elbows her in the side. "Yes, really."

"That's pretty thin."

"Yours don't touch."

"Yeah, well, if I want to get work, I have to show some daylight there." She swivels her hips. "Apparently, it's sexy."

"Bones work." Kas turns to inspect her butt.

Marin turns Kas back to face the mirror. "I think you're gorgeous just the way you are. But if you want to lose a few pounds, I'll help you. I know all the tricks."

Kas smiles at her in the mirror. "Can you make cinnamon toast disappear?"

"Hey, work with me. I'm not a magician."

Jacob meets her at the door, his face registering delight, then changing to concern. "I would have picked you up." He takes the grocery bags out of her hands. "These weigh a ton."

Mrs. Greene looks over her shoulder from the pot of potatoes she's peeling. "I just brought a load of groceries from the city. What did I miss?"

Jacob sets the bags on the counter. Kas hangs up her

coat and begins unpacking the bags. Jacob peers in the bags. "Did you shop at a store that sells only nonfat dressing?"

"I like the taste." Kas takes the dressing from him and puts it in the fridge.

"And nonfat yogurt. Nonfat cheese. Cheese is supposed to have fat in it. If you don't want to eat fat, then don't eat cheese. Personally, I'd like to eat cheese that tastes like cheese, not orange plastic." He reads the label on the jar he's holding. "Not nonfat mayo too!"

Mrs. Greene glances at a dairy carton. "Nonfat creamer. I'd like to try that."

Kas says to Jacob, "See, everyone uses this stuff." She crumples the grocery bags into a bin. "Oh, Mrs. Greene, I ate while I was out. Sorry I didn't phone."

Mrs. Greene shakes her head. "And I've peeled a mountain of potatoes too."

Jacob grins. "If Kas isn't eating, can I have hers?"

The air is so cold that it feels like a knife in her throat. Kas breathes it in, glad for the pain. Her legs are cold too, but she's sweating. Her running shoes crunch along the side of the road, the sidewalks long behind her. Some of the farmhouses still show lights; many are in darkness. The night is clear, the stars a light show. Just a little farther, then she'll turn. At the train tracks, she'll turn. At the next crossroads, she'll turn.

Just a little farther, then she'll turn.

Chapter Ten

Marin reaches into her backpack and pulls out a beat-up copy of *Macbeth*. "What I need you to do is read the other parts."

"I thought you were preparing the 'Out, damned spot' solo."

"Soliloquy. I am. Sometimes they ask for an additional reading, and this way I can practice my cues."

"The audition is almost two months away, isn't it? Won't you forget everything?"

"I'll practice over and over. I have to be perfect." She slips down onto the floor with her back against the bed. "Sit here so we can share the book."

Kas settles on the floor next to Marin. "What does it mean, anyway, when Lady Macbeth says, 'Out, damned spot'?"

Marin rubs her hands as if she's washing them. "She's trying to clean the blood off her hands, of the guys she and hubby Macbeth have murdered. Only there's no blood, only guilt, and she'll never get it off."

"She goes crazy?"

"Yes, but in a physically attractive way." Marin tosses her dark hair.

"Of course." Kas flips the book open, "That way we can feel sorry for her."

"Right. No one wants to watch a loser purging her guilt."

Kas glances at Marin. Marin says, "You're Macbeth. Read from here." She points to the place in the book.

Kas says, "Do you have to wear a costume for the audition?"

"No, thank goodness. I just have to look dead sexy. Mom's buying me a new dress." She points again to the text. "Go ahead."

Kas hesitates. "Don't laugh."

"Lady Macbeth would not do that to her friend." She nudges Kas in the side. "Read."

Kas takes a deep breath. When she reads, her voice quivers. She lowers the book with a sigh.

Marin shakes her head. "Just try to tap into a dark, murderous soul." She lifts the book again so that Kas can read. "Try putting on a fake voice. That might help."

Kas rumbles her voice.

"Excellent. Very manly."

She reads, then follows the lines as Marin reads. At the end of the scene, Marin says, "Oscar worthy."

Kas laughs.

Marin takes the book from her and pages to a bookmark. "Actually, that voice you used kind of creeped me out."

"Dark and murderous."

"Something." She flattens the book open at her scene. "Okay, you read as I recite. Tell me if I screw up a line." She hands the book to Kas, then gets to her feet. "It has to be perfect."

"Perfect. Oh, is that all?"

Chapter Eleven

On the other edge of town, Kas finds the municipality buildings. Road sanders enter and leave a large gated area. She spots Jacob's car parked next to a low building. When she stops panting, she can hear dogs barking. She jogs down the road to the shelter building and pushes open the door.

A woman wearing the same uniform as Jacob looks up from the front desk. She blinks.

Kas knows she looks ridiculous. Her ski hat is dusted with snow, her cheeks burning red with cold. It was a long run.

The woman, looking doubtful, says, "Can I help you?"

Her face is so cold it takes Kas two tries to make her mouth work. "Is Jacob here?"

Of course he's here, genius. His car is here.

"I mean, could I please talk to Jacob?"

The woman picks up the phone and, farther away in the building, Kas hears a phone ring. In a minute, Jacob walks out to the front desk. When he sees Kas, he breaks into a huge grin.

"I know. I'm a vision of beauty."

He touches her hair. "You're pure white."

Below her hat, her hair is coated with frost. She takes off her hat and snow plops onto the floor.

"Oops."

"Someone has to clean that up, you know." He laughs. "Did you run all the way out here? It's at least three miles."

She peels off her gloves. "It's not too far—just thought I'd say hello."

"I'm glad." He turns to the woman at the desk. "Okay if I take my break now?"

She nods.

To Kas he says, "Come on. I'll show you around."

Kas follows Jacob, and the sound of barking dogs grows louder. As they enter the dog kennels, a racket starts up with dogs jumping up against their chain-link enclosures. Kas retreats from the wire mesh.

"It's loud, I know. You get used to it." Jacob kneels beside an enclosure, and a dark-colored dog pants happily as he scratches its ears through the mesh. Kas stoops down beside Jacob.

"Don't you want to take them all home?" She puts her fingers through the mesh, and the dog licks them.

"They'll find homes."

Kas strokes the dog's ear. "This one looks nice and fat."

"She's pregnant."

"No way. Who would dump their pregnant dog?"

"Could be they just lost her." He gets to his feet. "She's

right where she needs to be. We have a vet on staff, and the mother will get great care. There's already a list of people who want her pups."

"And her?"

"Well, hopefully someone will take her too." He reaches down and offers Kas his hand.

The warmth of his hand surprises her—almost hot compared to her chilled bones. She laces her fingers through his, and he tugs her to her feet. She waits for him to drop her hand but he doesn't.

"Uh, Jacob, the dog was just licking my hand."

Jacob brings her hand to his mouth. "A little spit never hurt anything." He kisses her hand.

She's warm now, everywhere. "Tell me you don't kiss dogs."

He looks at her lips. "Never."

The dogs are going ballistic in their enclosures. He says, "I'll show you the rest of the place." He leads her back into the hallway. Just outside the kennel area, Kas stops him beside a door with a sign that reads, Staff Only. "What's in here?"

"Vet room." He tugs her hand to keep walking.

"Can I see it?"

"Not much to see."

It's too warm all of a sudden, as if she's stepped under a heater. "I'd like to."

Jacob toes a tile line on the floor. He speaks slowly,

quietly, as if he's talking to himself. "Not all the animals can be adopted."

Her stomach lurches.

He continues, "Some are just too sick or too screwed up. Some come in from the highway, hit by cars. Some are too old. They do their best."

"They kill them."

He nods. "They have to."

"I want to see it."

"There's nothing in there, really."

"So show me."

He shrugs, and pushes open the door.

The room is small—a stainless steel table in the middle, empty glass enclosures on each side, a large steel door ajar on one end. Kas can hear the dogs barking in another part of the building, but the sound is muffled.

Kas folds her arms against her chest. "How do they do it?"

Jacob points to the glass enclosures. "Gas. It makes the animals fall asleep, then kills them. The animals don't feel a thing."

"You don't think the animals know? Like, they can't smell all the dead animals before them?"

Jacob says, "Maybe they would die soon, anyway. At least they don't suffer." He touches Kas on the arm. "Are you okay? Do you want to leave?"

Kas shakes off his hand. "I'm fine." She points to the

steel door. "What is this?" She pulls on a metal lever to open the door. "It looks like a big pottery kiln."

Jacob moves to close the door. "Not quite."

Kas pulls the door open again. On the floor of the chamber a layer of gray ash lies inches thick. Kas lifts some ash between her fingers. She lets the ash fall. She points to a mound in the ash. On its side in the bedding of ash is a small rib cage.

Quietly, Jacob says, "It must be a cat."

For a long moment they both look at it.

Kas says, "If you touched it, would it crumble to dust?"

"You didn't have to drive me home."

"It's no big deal." Jacob has his windshield wipers on to clear the snow. It's cold in the car even with the heater blasting. He switches on the disc player.

"I have this one."

He smiles. "I know."

She draws the collar of her running jacket around her ears. "I shouldn't have bothered you at work."

He reaches over and thumps her lightly on the arm. "Bother me, please."

She sets her head back against the seat.

He says, "It's nice to see you smile."

She looks at him, watches as he drives. He hums to the tune.

"You're a happy person."

He glances at her. "I am now."

"Since coming to Whitchurch, you mean?"

"That too."

"Your parents give you a hard time for choosing music over engineering?"

He grins. "They say that math and music share a brain. They're still hoping that I'll come to my senses."

"My mother would love you. She tried for years to get me to take piano lessons. All I wanted to do was color."

"I'd like to meet your mother."

"You didn't mind all those hours of practicing?"

His fingers on the steering wheel tap out a melody on imaginary keys. "Never felt like work." He pulls a disc from the case beside him and hands it to her. "Put this one in."

One side of the disc is marked with his name. She loads it into the player and selects it to play. She hears piano music. "This is what you played for me?"

He nods.

She settles back in the seat and closes her eyes. "It's mine, right?"

"Yes."

The music washes around her. "It's beautiful, Jacob." She lifts her chin as if the music could pour like water into her ears. When the music finishes, she opens her eyes.

He glances from her to the road. "I'm writing lyrics for it." He pulls up outside of the house and parks the car.

She should get out. He has to go back to work. She undoes her seat belt.

"You're shivering. Come here." He pats the seat beside him and undoes his seat belt.

She slides across the seat. He puts his arm around her. "I should go in."

She feels his lips against her temple.

She tips her face. She smells aftershave. Mouthwash. His lips brush her cheek, her mouth.

Don't screw this up.

His eyes close and he kisses her.

Chapter Twelve

"Can I have one of those muffins or are you going to torture me with the aroma?"

Kas jumps at the sound of Jacob's voice. "What are you doing up so early?"

"I've got to go in early today. I'm working the sound booth."

She pushes the rack toward him. "They're low fat, so you'll need lots of butter."

He laughs. "Are you having one?"

"Already ate."

He breaks off the top of a muffin and spreads it with butter. The butter melts instantly. He takes a bite and closes his eyes. He polishes off that muffin and reaches for another. "Wheat bran. Sunflower seeds. What else did you put in?"

"Protein powder. My secret ingredient."

"Excellent. I feel stronger already." He butters a third. "You going running?"

She nods. "I'm meeting Marin. We're running before class."

"You want a ride to her house? I'll take you when I go."

"That's okay. I'll run to her house. It'll be my warm-up."

"I'm surprised Marin can keep up with you, she's such a twig."

Kas blinks.

And you're not, are you?

"Whose idea was this?" Marin closes her front door quietly and joins Kas, who is waiting on the sidewalk, jogging in place. It is still dark, the streetlight catching them in a blue-white pool. Their breath hangs like fog. Marin snugs the cuffs on her form-fitting running jacket. She stamps her feet and swings her arms. "It is freezing! It never seems this cold when we run in the evenings."

Kas bends to re-tie her running shoe. "You'll warm up once we get going."

"How do you know?"

Kas straightens up. "I woke up early and couldn't go back to sleep, so I did a short run."

"Already? You've had your workout then. We don't have to go."

"Nice try." Kas starts off at a slow jog. "You said you'd help me lose weight."

Marin sighs. "Fine." She steps in beside Kas. "I didn't count on freezing my lungs."

"I saw Jacob this morning." Kas's breath puffs little clouds.

"Did you spy on him in the shower? I would."

"Not spy. Observe. And no, I don't want to see what he does in the shower."

"So, did you say something?"

"Like, 'Good morning'?"

"No. Like, 'Hi. I want to have your baby.'"

"I said, 'Good morning.' *He* said, 'Hi. I'd like to have your baby.'"

"It must be the Krispy Kreme hat with the knit headband, and the highly attractive plaid scarf." Marin flips the brim on Kas's hat. "Does your dad know you have his scarf? But full makeup, I see. You do have standards."

"Yeah, well. Sorry I didn't deep condition my hair."

Marin arranges her headband around her dark sheaf of hair and laughs. "It's too bad we have to work so hard to look so good."

"Jacob doesn't. He eats anything and everything."

"And he is one fine specimen."

Kas peers at her from under the brim of her cap. "Based on what he looks like in clothes, you mean?"

Marin prods her in the arm. "No. Based on the wild sex we had." She shakes her head. "Give me credit for some imagination."

Kas shrugs. "Imagination. That's all I'm working with."

"So far."

Now Kas laughs.

Marin says, "Imagine we could eat all day and all night, and when we ran in the morning, we wouldn't leave tracks in the snow."

"Imagine."

Kas's knee is throbbing. With each step she counts off the calories.

Burn. Breathe. Burn.

Chapter Thirteen

Kas knows every panel in Jacob's bedroom door. He closes it when he goes to bed, and when she's sure he's asleep, she stands at the door, listening to him.

When she was a little kid, she played hide and seek. The entire neighborhood played after supper in the summertime—a horde of kids of all ages. She remembers hiding in a willow thicket, standing motionless among the trees. In her bare feet, sticky sap glued her in place, holding her so that she couldn't move. The boy who was *It* paused not five feet away from her. She was sure he was looking right at her face, but he didn't speak, and after a long moment, he ran on. She could be so close to him and yet be invisible, and that both freaked her out and excited her.

In hide and seek, she was never caught. Not once. Some evenings, she hid in the same spot the entire time, never coming out. She never revealed her hiding places to her friends, and she never hid with another person. It seemed to her that if they stopped looking for her—even when her friends were *It*—she had successfully become invisible.

Jacob is closer than that, but of course, the door is between them. A solid wooden door. Does she only imagine that she can hear him breathing? She wants to move away from the door, but it's as if she's frozen to it. She's afraid to blink in case he hears her and knows that she's listening to him. If he knew she was standing here, would he call to her? Would she open his door and go in?

If she stills her own breath, will she hear his?

She's invisible. In this house, she is invisible.

Maybe, if she looked in the mirror right now, she wouldn't appear. Her time here would crumble away and with each breath Jacob took, she would vaporize. All sign of her, all sense, would vanish so that when Jacob woke up, he wouldn't know she'd even been here. And she'd be frozen in time's amber casket. Invisible.

Chapter Fourteen

Marin raises her feet up a rung on the art room stool. She sips from a cup of cafeteria tea that she holds in one hand while she flips through a fashion magazine with the other. Only one other table in the art room is occupied—a younger student working with Mr. Randall. The teacher's lunch bag is open on the table, and he eats a sandwich as he gestures to the student's work.

Kas says, "Do fashion models always turn their faces from the camera?"

Marin says, "That's how she hides her flaws," Marin points to a model's face, "or shows off her perfect bones."

Kas eats a spoonful of yogurt. "Yours are better."

"You need to get your eyes checked." Marin sets her face in the same pose as the model. "If she shows both sides of her face, she reveals too much of herself. And everyone has something to hide."

Kas shifts on her stool. She pushes the yogurt aside and picks up a translucent film canister. She taps the canister and fine ash sifts down the insides of the container.

Marin says, "I can't believe you actually took that. What did Jacob say?"

"Jacob didn't see me. I went in when he was busy in the kennels."

"You stole them behind his back?"

"I didn't steal them. I took them. I didn't tell him because I didn't want him to think I'm weird."

Marin rolls her eyes. "At least you realize you're weird. That's good."

"It's not that weird. People do it. It's called an essence, when you have just a tiny bit of someone's ashes."

"That looks like more than a tiny bit."

"There was more than one animal in there."

"So, you have a tiny bit of several animals. Now what?"

Kas turns the canister in her hands. "I'm going to set them free." She places the canister on her art room desk and smooths a fresh sheet of paper onto the surface. She selects a piece of charcoal and draws a fine black edge to the profile of a figure. Her hands work quickly, forming the outline—a woman, her legs drawn up on a stool, her head tilted so that the light catches the angles of her cheeks. With her finger, Kas feathers the outline, softening it. She reaches for the canister and opens it, extracts a pinch of ash in her fingers, and places it in her open palm. Using her palm as a palette, her finger as a brush, she rubs the ash to fine gray, then she presses her fingertip to the surface of the drawing.

"You can see your fingerprint in the ash."

Kas moves to brush away the marks.

"No," Marin says, "it looks good that way, tiny lines between the lines. Give me the drawing, and when you're old and famous, I'll sell it and get rich."

"You'll be old too. What are you going to do with a pile of money?"

Marin says, "I'll open a school for aspiring actors. They'll worship me."

"Van Gogh was dead and buried before he sold a painting."

"Don't wait that long."

Kas applies more charcoal, drawing a fall of hair over one side of the figure's face. Kas leaves this line starkly black, then uses fine strokes to fill in the hair.

"She's got great hair. And that body!"

Kas pauses, looks at Marin. "You're a good model."

Marin leans closer to Kas's worktable. "That's not me."

"It is."

Marin glances over at Mr. Randall. "Then I want clothes."

"I haven't shown anything." With a light touch, Kas shadows the hollow in the figure's collarbone. "The way she's sitting, she could be wearing a strapless swimsuit."

Marin studies the drawing. "She's thinner than me. More graceful."

Kas smiles. "When researchers asked women if they thought they were beautiful, something like only two percent thought they were."

Kas takes the drawing to the art room counter as Marin follows her. She sprays a fixative over the drawing, then sets it to dry.

Marin says, "Your fingerprint, it looks kind of like an aura behind my head. I look like a dark angel."

Kas examines the drawing. "You're seeing things."

"You didn't sign it."

"My name is on the back."

"You never sign your artwork."

Kas shrugs, then tips her head toward the art teacher. "He knows whose they are."

Chapter Fifteen

"Who would let their pregnant dog languish in the pound?"

"I don't think her owner is looking for her." Jacob pushes the mop back and forth over the hallway tile. "The vet says she's had pups before—several litters. Probably her owner got tired of selling pups in the classifieds."

"So the owner just left her to fend for herself? That's humane." Kas stays just ahead of Jacob, setting her feet into the tile squares so that she doesn't touch the lines. "You think she misses her owner?"

"She might have at first. She wouldn't know that she was being abused. She'd think it was normal."

"Because she didn't know any different."

"Even if she didn't like it a lot, it was all she knew."

"And she stuck with what she knew because anything else was too scary."

He dunks his mop in the bucket, watching her. "Exactly."

When he looks at her like that, it's as if he is looking into her. She turns away from his gaze.

He says, "I swear, you and I think the same way."

She laughs. "Be afraid."

"When I first saw you, it was as if I already knew you."

She hops on one foot between the tile squares. "When I first saw you, I knew I liked you." She stops, holds her breath.

"Yes, you did say that out loud."

Kas feels her face burning.

He says, "I liked you too, right from the start."

She breathes.

He says, "I'm just about done here. Want to go grab a coffee?"

She looks at him. He smiles. The feeling rushes over her: she more than likes him. Her mouth is suddenly dry. "Coffee sounds good."

He wrings out the mop. "I'll put this away. Give me a few minutes, and I'll be right with you."

Kas studies her pale reflection in the floor that Jacob has just washed. She stretches her hands over her head, turning her shoulder and hip to minimize her width. Down the hall, Jacob disappears with the bucket and mop. His absence feels abrupt, and for a disconcerting moment, she feels that he won't be back. She turns, watching her reflection, straining over her shoulder to see herself, spinning her head so that she can keep looking.

Chapter Sixteen

Marin takes the text of *Macbeth* from Kas and says, "Thanks for letting me come over. My dad said he'd read with me, but you're way better." She checks her watch. "Ooh, it's late. I hope you don't have more work to do tonight."

Kas stretches. "I've got to work on my still life. I can't seem to make apples, oranges, and bananas say something to me beyond *fruit salad*." She yawns.

"You should switch to acting. It's way less work."

"Oh, yeah. The world is screaming for a fat female actor."

"Oh, please. You are not fat."

"You are a good actor."

"I won't even dignify that comment." Marin flops down on the bed. "Hey, you want to go into the city with me to buy an audition dress? We can catch a movie too."

"Do you have to wear a dress to the audition?"

"You just have to wear something that doesn't add bulk. I'd wear Saran Wrap if I thought it would pare an inch off my hips."

"Women used to wrap themselves in plastic to lose weight."

"That wouldn't work. They might sweat a pound of water but it would be right back as soon as they had anything to drink." Marin pauses, then lifts her eyebrows. "Speaking of Saran Wrap—are you doing any nude modeling for anyone?" She motions with her thumb toward Jacob's room.

Kas pushes her door closed. "Would you like a microphone? Some of the neighbors didn't quite hear."

Marin lowers her voice to a whisper. "He really likes you. He told me you went for coffee after work and didn't get home until midnight." She lifts her eyebrows. "Long time to be sitting in a coffee shop."

"That's all we did."

"Sat and drank coffee?"

"And talked."

"Talked."

"Yes, Marin. Some people just sit and talk."

She shrugs. "If you say so. What did you talk about?"

"Music. Art. Life."

"Fascinating. Did you kiss?"

"Duh. But that's it."

"Are you saving yourself?"

Kas laughs. "It feels good to talk. I can talk to him about anything, and he gets it."

"He'd probably like to get something more." Marin grins. "If I were you, I'd do less talking." With an audible sigh, Marin stretches out on Kas's bed and folds one arm behind her head, one over her forehead.

Kas grabs her sketchbook and flips it open to a clean page. "Don't move. That is a great pose." She makes some quick pencil lines on the page.

"The pups will be born soon." Kas's gaze moves from Marin to her sketchbook. "The vet says the mother has had pups before, but of course she doesn't know how the pups did."

"Yeah. Maybe the mother ate them."

"I don't think dogs eat their young."

"If my mother were a dog, she would."

"I don't think your mother is that bad."

"She likes you too. She says you're a good girl."

"Maybe I should take up acting. I must have a gift for it." She studies the drawing, then says, "Have a look."

Marin sits up and takes the sketchbook from Kas. "Eew. My gut is hanging out. You should have told me to pull my shirt down." She holds the page closer and squints. "Are those my ribs? You can't really see my ribs."

"Who is the artist here? I draw what I see."

"Must have been because I was stretched out." She tilts her head one way, then the other. "I look pretty good, actually."

"You do look good, Marin. You're going to rock at your audition."

A small shadow crosses Marin's eyes. "I hope so. What if I don't get the part?"

"You know your lines inside out. You'll be fine."

"Sometimes I think it would be better not to try. Then I can't be disappointed."

"Right. Nothing like risk-free anonymity." Kas rips the drawing from the pad of paper and hands it to Marin. "Here. So you remember how beautiful you are."

Marin takes the drawing. "You didn't sign it."

Kas sighs, takes the drawing, and pens her name in one corner.

"It's a very small signature."

Kas makes a motion to grab the picture back. Marin says, "But it's perfect." She sets the drawing on the desk.

Kas closes the sketchbook and tosses it in a drawer. She picks up the vial of ashes, dabs her finger, then rubs it on her cheek.

"Oh, that's nice." Marin wrinkles her nose.

Kas checks her reflection in the mirror, and then applies more ash to the other cheek.

"I'm not kidding, Kas. That is too disgusting."

"I think it makes me look sculpted."

"It makes you look dead."

Kas tilts her head to the side, to see the effect better. Taking a stub of charcoal from her desk, she darkens the lines of ash on her cheeks. "You want me to do you?"

Marin shifts onto her elbow. "You have anything other than animal ash and death-mask black?"

Kas opens her desk drawer and takes out a small cardboard box held closed with a rubber band. "Pastels." She removes the lid and shows Marin the contents: twelve slim paper-wrapped sticks of color.

Marin sits up, smooths the hair back from her face. "Paint me."

"What about your pores?"

Marin closes her eyes. "I'll cleanse. Go ahead; make me faaaabulous."

Kas pulls her desk chair close to Marin's knees. Taking Marin's chin in her hands, she turns Marin's face first one way, then the other. "Your face is almost totally symmetrical."

"Thanks, I think."

"It's not that common. Usually, the two sides are slightly different. Sometimes it's like two people welded down the center into one."

"My right foot is a half-size bigger than the left. My mother actually took me to an orthopedic surgeon to see if it could be corrected."

"You could just wrap the bigger foot—stunt it like Chinese women used to do to their feet."

"Lovely."

Kas tips Marin's face toward the light and strokes on a band of indigo. She matches the line exactly on the other cheek. She unwraps the paper from a deep purple and applies a wider band under the indigo, swirling the lines to follow the curve of Marin's cheekbones. Between these lines she pencils a thin strand of goldenrod. The pastel glides over Marin's skin. "It looks a little like war paint."

"Sounds good. Keep going."

"What if it makes you break out?"

"Hmm. Maybe I'll break out in colors."

"Who would your mother kill first—me or you?"

"Death by emotional tirade. It won't be quick."

"She believes in you, Marin. Maybe you should too."

"I'm realistic. If I can't deliver, then why try?"

"I think you set too high a standard for yourself."

"You're one to talk—still working on your still life."

Kas dots a line of cobalt blue along Marin's jaw, shading each dot so it appears like a tiny sphere. With white pastel, she marks the light. Then she swoops a tiny comet tail on each sphere using a silvery gray. "It isn't coming together for me."

"Ah, ha. You're the one with impossibly high standards." She pouts out her lips. "Do my mouth too."

"Maybe that's why we're friends." Kas uses a metallic blue-green and traces Marin's mouth. She sniffs the end of the pastel. "I wonder if these things might be toxic."

"I'm wearing them, not eating them."

"Check it out."

Marin opens her eyes, moves so that she can look in the mirror. She gasps. "I love this look. Take my picture." She rummages in her purse and hands Kas a small digital camera. "Take a picture of us both." She slides in next to Kas so that their images fill the mirror.

Kas runs her fingers over her cheeks. "I do look like death."

"You should paint your face too." Marin reaches for the pastels.

Kas lifts the camera to look through the viewfinder, then turns and snaps Marin's picture. Captured in the camera display is Marin in painted profile, she and her reflection in the mirror, gazing down.

Marin takes the camera from her and looks at the display. "Where are you? I thought you were taking both of us."

"I'm there. I'm like the eyes of the photo."

"It's good, Kas. I wish you were in the shot, though."

"You should probably wash that stuff off your face. I'm not sure if it stains."

Marin studies herself in the mirror. "I wouldn't mind."

"Your mother might."

Chapter Seventeen

Jacob is coming down the stairs as Kas goes up. He says, "Been out for a run already?"

Six miles. Her knee is throbbing. She shakes her head. "Just a warm-up. I'm heading out again."

"I'll go with you."

She laughs, and his face falls. He says, "You don't think I can do it. You don't think I can run."

She looks at him—at his jeans, at his huge skate shoes—and says, "Have you ever run?"

"Of course. Everybody runs."

She gives him a look.

He shrugs. "How hard can it be?" Then he grins.

"Some people start by walking."

"I walk."

"As far as your car."

"Kas, you wound me."

"You haven't had your breakfast yet. What if you expire from lack of food?"

He gets down on one knee. "Being with you will sustain me."

"You're spending too much time in Performing Arts."

He clasps his hands over his heart.

She laughs. "Fine. But you can't run in those." She points to his shoes.

He jumps up and plants a big kiss on her cheek. "I'll be right down."

Kas is stretching on the step when Jacob emerges from the house. He's wearing his jeans, but over these he's put on a pair of gray gym shorts. Kas sees three colors of sweatshirt at his wrists. He looks like a Technicolor marshmallow. He's wearing a knit headband, and his hair is pushed up beneath it so that his head looks square. On his feet, Jacob has put on a pair of Adidas, flattened and curling up slightly at the toes.

She tries not to laugh. "And I thought my running gear was unconventional."

"Anyone can wear spandex tights and Dri-fit. It takes a real man to wear Wranglers."

"Marin would refuse to run with us."

"Ha. She's just afraid we'd beat her." He starts down the sidewalk, his arms pumping purposefully.

She sets out after him. "Don't you want to warm up?"

"Warming up is for wimps." His breath explodes in clouds on the February morning air.

She falls into step next to him. "We'll start with a loop around the block and see how you're doing."

He snorts. "Around the block? Let's head out to the animal shelter."

She looks at him. His cheeks are already bright red. "Uh, Jacob, I was just planning a short run this morning. My knee has been bugging me."

"You turn around whenever you need to." He picks up his pace.

"How about if we go up to the highway—we can have a trucker breakfast."

"Nice try, Kas. Come on. You're slowing me down."

She lopes easily beside him. "It's slightly uphill toward the shelter. You don't really notice it when you drive."

"No problem," he pants.

"You're doing great."

He turns to her and grins. "Want to race?"

"Uuuugh," Jacob moans, his bare feet propped up on a bed pillow, ice bags on both shins. He's showered, and his hair hangs damply on his forehead.

Kas hands him a plate of scrambled eggs and toast. "Mrs. Greene thinks you should have something more than Advil for breakfast." She tries not to smile.

"I can't even lift my arms."

She sits down on the bed beside him. She loads a piece of toast with some eggs and holds it to his mouth. "Here. Try a bite."

He leans forward, grimacing with the effort, and eats it. "You didn't tell me it would hurt so bad."

"I tried."

"Even my hair is sore."

She smooths it back from his face. "We're lucky the shelter truck passed us when it did." She had flagged it down and the driver had taken them home. Jacob had wanted to crawl into the back where they put the dogs, but the driver had insisted he sit in the cab with a seat belt. It took both her and the driver to hoist him into the seat.

"I'm going to die, Kas."

"Not yet."

"I want to die."

"No, you don't."

He flexes his fingers. "Hey, I can still move my hands." He strokes the side of her face.

She laces her fingers with his. "You don't want to die, Jacob."

"I was joking."

"Don't joke—not about that."

He brings her hand to his mouth and kisses it. "Ouch. My lips hurt too." He blinks his eyes. "Kiss them better."

She laughs.

He tugs her down beside him. "Don't worry; I can't make a move on you. I'm practically paralyzed." He brushes his lips against hers.

It astonishes her, the rush of heat that floods from his lips, over hers, down her shoulders and torso. She catches a gasp in her throat. He smiles, then she watches his eyes close. She feels her lips part and feels him kissing her.

Kissing her. Tiny fires erupt under her skin. She closes her eyes. Gently, she presses her lips against his, amazed at the heat, at the oneness, at how complete she feels with him. Under her lips, he moans.

She pulls back. "Am I hurting you?"

He opens his eyes and grins. "Oh, no." The smile fades from his eyes, and his eyebrows crease with concern. "Are you okay? You look as if you want to cry."

She laughs. "I've never been better."

He wraps his arms around her, and she rests her head on his chest. She says, "I can hear your heart."

"It's a good one. Never been broken."

She traces his sternum with her fingers. She says, "For the first time since I arrived, I feel warm."

He kisses the top of her head. "You are perfectly wonderful." He's quiet for a moment, then he says, "I don't want to wreck things for us."

"You can't."

"I can. I know I can. I don't want it to happen with us."

"Jacob, I'm not going to rush you. I've never even…"

"I just mean that I want it to be perfect—for you. I know it'll be perfect for me. It's about all I can think about."

"So, we'll wait."

"We'll wait."

"For everything?"

She senses the shift in his breathing. "Oh, I hope not."

Chapter Eighteen

Kas peers into the box that the shelter staff set up for the mother dog. She counts the pups—tiny black and white bundles, their eyes closed as they nuzzle their mother's side. "Seven. A perfect number."

Jacob had called the shelter at lunch, to find out if the pups had been born. He had said he'd take her to see them when he went to work, but she couldn't wait. She had walked to the shelter right after classes.

The shelter vet, a young-looking grandmother-type with stylish gray hair and smiling eyes, scratches the mother dog behind the ears and says, "She's an old pro."

"She looks pleased with herself."

"She's got milk. That's good—enough for all these hungry rascals."

The pups push at her sides, coaxing the milk.

Kas says, "What kind are they?"

The vet laughs. "Well, let's see. The mother looks like a chow-shepherd mix, and with their coloring the pups appear to have some black Lab. Let's call them mutts."

Kas sits down on the floor beside the box. "Why isn't that one eating?" She points to an all-black pup.

The vet reaches in and tucks the pup closer to its mother. "She's too little for us to know for certain. Maybe you'd like to try her with a bottle?"

Kas's eyes widen. "I would."

The vet gets up and goes over to the counter. "Come here. I'll show you how to mix the formula."

Kas watches as she works. "It needs to be as warm as the pup—blood temperature, it's called. Some people use the microwave, but I like warm water." She clips a thermometer onto the bottle, and then sets the bottle into a flask of warm water. Finally, the vet removes the bottle, snaps on a nipple, and hands it to Kas. "I'll bring her to you. Get comfortable."

Kas sets herself on a chair. "I'm all tingly."

The vet calls over her shoulder, "Grab a clean towel in case she pees."

The vet hands Kas the pup.

"Oh!"

"Are you all right?" The vet puts her hands out for the pup.

"No. I mean, I'm totally okay. It's just that she's so small." Kas studies the black pup. Her eyes are closed, and her tiny ears are petals folded close to her head. She nestles in the cup of Kas's hands, round and warm—the pink skin on her belly almost translucent in its newness. In her hands the pup squirms, and Kas feels miniature claws on her palms.

The vet smiles at her. "I know. I never get tired of seeing new pups." The vet positions the pup on the towel and snugs the bundle close in to Kas. "There you are, sweet girl. Kas has something you'll like." She helps Kas position the bottle. The pup noses the nipple, tastes it, and then takes it in her mouth. The vet croons, "Good girl."

Kas can't take her eyes from the tiny pup she holds. It stretches out on its tummy, pulling eagerly on the bottle. "She's drinking!"

"Talk quietly to her, encourage her to drink up."

Kas leans over the pup. "Good girl. Good puppy."

"I'll be back. You're doing a great job."

Kas feels a flush of pride. She hears the vet sigh, then the door clicks closed.

Chapter Nineteen

"You're going to ruin your manicure. And don't tug at your hair. You'll get breakage." Kas sits back in her desk chair. Marin is wound into a knot at the end of Kas's bed, chewing her thumb and twisting a length of hair with her other hand.

"Ha, ha. You sound just like my mother." Marin buries her face under her arm.

Kas shakes her head. "For someone so good at theatrics, I'm amazed you're second-guessing the audition."

"Ugh." Marin flops over onto her back. "I can't do it. They'll never give me the part." She rolls up to a sitting position. "It's just so fake. I don't know what old lady Macbeth is feeling. How do you get inside the head of someone so screwed up?"

Kas sets down the sketchbook she was working in. "You don't have to kill someone to know how awful you'd feel afterward."

Marin sighs. "That's what makes it hard. The audience wants her normal, yes, but also perfect—and perfectly deranged."

"Two characters in one."

"Yes."

"What happens to Lady Macbeth in the end?"

"Her guilty conscience gets her. She kills herself."

"So, the guilty conscience is the good guy, right...the white angel on her shoulder?"

Marin shrugs.

"So, find the thing inside her that makes her murderous."

"The little red guy with horns."

Kas nods. "You've got to have the two duke it out. Show the battle between good and evil; bring the lady to her knees."

Kas opens a desk drawer and pulls out a lined school scribbler. She flips it open to a crayoned picture.

Marin says, "Looks like some early work."

Kas smiles. "I only knew from my mother's reaction that this drawing was good." She holds it so Marin can see. "I was in first grade."

Marin whistles. "Girl in a ponytail. Big green eyes. Must be you."

Kas nods.

Marin leans closer to the drawing. "What's that covering her mouth? It looks like a man's hand."

"It is."

Marin draws back. "Yuck."

"You should have seen my mother's face. She thought someone was messing with me. But look." She points to the crayoned lines. "It's her own hand."

"Nice, Kas. God. Most six-year-olds draw flowers and houses."

"Evocative, no?"

"And slightly twisted."

"Aren't we all? Anyway, that's when Mom started enrolling me in art classes."

"As a form of therapy, no doubt."

Kas laughs. "Come on. Even an actor can see the raw talent in this drawing." She tosses the scribbler back in the drawer. "Your Lady Macbeth has something dark inside her, or…I don't know…maybe she thinks she's basically evil, and that's why she kills herself. The point is that the two sides are always in conflict."

"Fairly literate, for an artist."

"Thank you."

"Everything makes sense now." Marin narrows her eyes elaborately. "About you, anyway."

Kas crosses her arms. "Oh?"

Marin nods. "You're good, but you think you're bad."

Kas holds her breath.

"And that's why you second-guess everything you draw for Mr. Randall."

Kas throws up her hands in imitation of Marin. "Why turn it in if it's just going to fail?"

"You don't know it's going to fail."

"You don't know you're not going to get the part."

"Why should I try? Why is it okay for you not to try,

but I have to put myself out there—actual body, actual soul?"

"It's not the same, Marin. You have real talent."

"Oh, my. You sound so much like my mother."

"Maybe you should be having this conversation with your mother."

"Okay, enough. Who are you and what have you done with Kas?"

"Go to the audition. We'll find you a dead-sexy dress. They'll fall all over themselves signing you."

"But—"

"You'll get the role. And on opening night, I'll be your biggest fan."

Chapter Twenty

She's sick. Half the school has the flu, and she must have caught it. It's been a long time; she'd forgotten the feeling, the reversing floodgate, vomit up and out. Ugh. The taste is awful. Spit and flush; turn off the water. Kas studies her reflection in the mirror. She looks pale. She puts her hand on her forehead, like her mother did to check for fever.

Idiot. You can't feel your own temperature.

She opens Jacob's mouthwash, takes a swig, swishes until the burning makes her eyes water. Spits. Rinses the sink.

She feels a little better, as if some of the poison is out of her.

Kas rolls back into her bed. She imagines that she hears her mother's voice. *It doesn't make sense to go to school when you're sick, Kas. If you stay home, you'll get better faster.* In fifth grade she went an entire school year without missing a day, even when half the class had the flu so bad they missed a week of school. Not her. She wanted the certificate the school gave out at the awards ceremony for perfect attendance. She wanted that and the citizenship award, and the award for outstanding scholastic achievement, *and* the athlete of the year award. But that year they didn't give out the perfect attendance awards. It wouldn't be fair, they said, because of the flu.

When the Greenes leave for work, she'll get up and have a little breakfast. She'll make weak tea. That's what her mother would make for her, weak tea with sugar and milk. And plain toast. No butter. Not on a sick stomach.

Jacob is already gone.

Kas turns her pillow over to the cool side. When will they leave?

She hears their car start. Kas peeps through the blinds to see Mr. Greene on the street, brushing the snow from the car as it warms up. The snow looks heavy and wet. Kas hears the front door open and close, then sees Mrs. Greene stepping through the snow to the car. She waves to someone in a passing car. Don't they have to get going? Mr. Greene opens the door for her, then goes around the car, flicking bits of snow off the bumper with the snow brush. Finally, he gets in and closes his door.

It's weird, watching them, with them not knowing.

Mrs. Greene looks back at the house, and Kas's heart stops for an instant, but she doesn't look up to Kas's window. The car pulls away from the curb. They're going. Kas watches them drive up the street. She watches the flash of their signal light, watches them turn up toward the highway. She watches until she can't see them anymore, then watches a minute longer, making herself wait. Then she goes to the kitchen.

Chapter Twenty-one

"Just a few more minutes, Kas. I have to lock up." Mr. Randall sits back in his chair and stretches. Outside, it's dark and snowing. "Mrs. R. will be calling the hospitals."

Kas glances at the clock. She'll have missed supper again. Her stomach grumbles angrily. She steps off her stool and removes a mirror she had propped on her workstation. "I had no idea it was this late. I'm sorry."

"You were so intent that I didn't want to break your concentration." He gets up. "Will you show me your portrait?"

She shrugs. "It's not finished."

He makes his way to her workstation. He looks at the drawing, tilting his head, his hand stroking his chin. His eyebrows knit, his lips tighten.

She says, "I probably shouldn't bother finishing it. It's trash."

He shakes his head. "No." He picks up the drawing and studies it. "It's unusual for a self-portrait to have two subjects."

"They're both me."

"I can see that."

"The one in the mirror is my reflection."

"Uh huh." He sets down the drawing. "But it's not quite you."

"I worked from my image in the mirror. Doesn't it look like me?"

He waits a moment before speaking. "It does, but there's something different about her." He takes a pencil out of his shirt pocket and taps the eraser end on the drawing. "See, here, how her eyes are looking down, as if she's looking down on the other girl. She's the reflection, yet she's in a superior position."

"I'm sorry, Mr. Randall. I thought I drew them exactly the same."

"It's not a criticism, Kas, just a comment." He leans closer to the drawing. "The set of her eyes is different, harder somehow. Almost dark."

Kas sweeps her equipment into her pack. "Maybe there is something to that theory that everyone has an evil twin."

"Doppelganger Syndrome." He straightens. "Could be because you were working from the mirror. It's good work, though. I'm glad to see you got it finished."

Unlike the still life.

He says, "I marked the charcoal you did of your friend." He goes to his desk and sifts through a pile of work, extracting the picture of Marin sitting on the art stool. He shows her the mark. "Five out of five."

Kas feels her cheeks flush.

He says, "It's an excellent drawing, Kas. One of the best I've seen from a student."

She zips up her pack. "Marin's a terrific model. She'd make my little sister's art look good."

He leans against her workstation. "Why are you at Whitchurch, Kas?"

"Because I want to be an artist."

"Just an artist?"

"No." She puts on her coat and shoulders her pack. "I want to be good. Really good."

"One of the best?"

"I doubt that."

"You can be, Kas. But you're not there yet."

"I know. I'm not good at all."

Mr. Randall raises his hands. "Let me finish. This is exactly what I'm talking about. You're incredibly gifted. Exceptionally driven. I have no doubt you can be what you want to be. But if you're going to know you're good, then you have to step back from yourself, see yourself as others see you."

She makes a move to grab the drawing on her workstation, but he puts his hand on her wrist.

Tears prick at her eyes. "I'll re-do it at home."

"You've spent hours on this, and it's good. Sign it and turn it in." Gently, he pulls the drawing away from her. He hands her his pencil. "Sign it."

Blinking back tears, she scribbles her name in the corner.

"Thank you." He takes the portrait and the charcoal of Marin, and sets them on his desk. "Will someone come to pick you up? It's miserable tonight."

She shakes her head. "I can use the walk."

He takes his coat from the back of his chair and holds the studio door open for her. "Whitchurch is lucky to have you here, Kas."

She steps past him into the hall. "I'm the lucky one."

Kas sits on the front steps of the school. Snow is starting to pile up on her coat and bag. Inside the school, Kas watches the custodian as he mops the floor around the Vortex sculpture. He knocks the sculpture with his mop handle, and it starts a slow spin. She looks away as she talks into her cell phone. No one picked up when she called home. Out with her sisters, maybe. She speaks to the answering machine.

"…it's unheard of. Mr. Randall never gives full marks. I used to think the teachers at home marked tough until I met Mr. Randall. He loved it. I wouldn't be surprised if he hangs it in the front hall of the school. He's hard, you know, but he gets me to really examine my art. He pushes me to make it that much better. Everyone should be able to study with teachers like Mr. Randall. Already he's raised the bar for me, and I'll do it, for him, I'll be that much better. Am I going on and on? Sorry. I'm just so pumped. Tell everyone I say hello. Tell everyone I love them." She flips the phone closed.

She's cold now, as if she's frozen to the stone steps of the school. She puts her phone away and straightens up.

Walk. Burn some lard.

Blackness darts in front of her eyes, and she sways until it clears. Lightheaded. It must be from watching that sculpture spin. Kas blinks, takes a deep breath, then picks her way down the steps. The streets are empty; everyone is home from work. The snow is new on the sidewalks so she walks in the road, leaving her tracks where someone will drive by and erase them.

Chapter Twenty-two

Jacob tips the wastebasket in Kas's room with his foot and whistles. "You must really like Diet Pepsi."

An empty can rolls from the top of the heaped wastebasket. She stoops to pick it up and lobs it back in. "Want one?" She pushes the window blind aside to reveal a case of Diet Pepsi. "It's my personal fridge."

"Got anything real?"

"For a treat, on Sundays. If I'm very, very good."

He laughs. "And if you're not?"

She snuggles next to him on the bed. "Bread and water."

He buries his nose in the nape of her neck. "I could live on bread and water, so long as I have you."

She laughs. "The way you eat, you wouldn't last a week."

"Try me."

She rests her head on his shoulder. "Do you think you have an exact double somewhere?"

"If I do, I hope he's found your exact double."

"I don't deserve you."

Kas feels tired suddenly, her entire body like lead.

Jacob yawns. She says, "When I go to bed, will you play me something on your keyboard?"

"I'll wake up the whole house."

"Play it softly so that only I can hear it."

He wraps her into a hug. "Classic rock or hip-hop?"

"Something you wrote."

His lips are on her temple, and he kisses her. "For someone I'm crazy about."

"Jacob—"

He puts his finger on her lips. "Don't say it. Don't say anything." He turns her chin toward him and kisses her. "Just know that I am."

MARCH

MARCH

Chapter Twenty-three

The coffee shop on the highway is almost empty. It's way too early for the morning crowd; anyone here is pulling an all-nighter. Kas drops her pack on a chair. Across from her, a man sits huddled over a cup of coffee. He's wearing a hat pulled down hard to his ears. His face doesn't look old, but below the hat Kas sees that the man is bald except for stray strands of hair. His neck bones stand out like knuckles. He's wearing headphones, and Kas can hear his music. Good music. She settles in her seat and opens her math book.

She counts the calories she ate for the day, then she counts them again to be sure she didn't miss any. The server comes. Kas orders, "Coffee, black."

She studies the man's profile. His skin is pale with a yellow undertone. It stretches smooth over his cheekbones. No wrinkles. Not old, but very, very thin. She turns to her own reflection in the coffee-shop window. Dark shadows circle both eyes. She looks like her mother. With a shudder, she turns from the glass.

An apple. Eighty. Nonfat yogurt, but only half the container. Fifty. Celery. Carrot sticks. Two slices of low-cal bread. Another eighty. Nonfat cheese. Nonfat mayo. Ice water doesn't count. *But water weighs something, and it puffs you up.*

The man reminds her of Jacob, but it's not Jacob. Of course, it's not. He turns and catches her looking at him. She cranks her eyes back to the window.

You didn't count the muffin you bought in the cafeteria.

It wasn't a whole muffin, it was just a bite.

But you didn't count it, and now you've gone over.

The window is like a movie screen, and she watches herself in it—as if she's watching the action play out from a seat in the audience.

In the window, Kas catches the man's reflection, his face looking at hers in the reflection of his own window. It startles her, but he doesn't detect her yet. He seems to be studying her, as if he knows her from somewhere. His reflected eyes seem yearning, as if he's hungry too. He sees her then and drops his gaze. In the window glass, she watches herself watching the man, somewhere else, watching herself with the man.

Chapter Twenty-four

Kas opens her eyes, closes them, and then tries once more to focus. The Wellness teacher shoves his way into the circle of girls looking down on her.

"There are three of you," she says to him.

He looks scared. "Don't move."

"I'm fine." Kas tries to lift herself to her elbows. She tugs her sweatshirt down lower, over her gym pants. He puts his hands on her shoulders. He watches her, but asks the others, "How high up was she when she fell?"

Marin elbows away the other girls and says, "She was halfway to the ceiling. She said she wanted to ring the bell."

Kas smiles. She is a fallen leaf in the forest, light strata, compressing under time. Umber. Ochre. Black.

Girls giggle. One mutters, "Stoner."

Black leaves decomposing, worms digesting. *Dirt.*

"I rang *my* bell. Hey, Marin, you look like you're in a three-way mirror."

When Dr. Bowen comes in, Kas is sitting with her legs crossed, one foot tapping the air.

"That was quite the fall, young lady." He turns, reads the weight his assistant entered on her chart, nods. "Have you been sick?"

A black curtain closes briefly over her eyes, and she blinks. "I had a touch of the flu. Half the school has it."

He stands close to her, palpating the glands in her neck.

"I'm fine now."

"Stick out your tongue." He places a wooden depressor on her tongue. "Say 'Ahhh.'" He shines a light onto the back of her throat. "Is your throat sore?"

"A bit."

He nods. "It looks a little raw." He steps back, makes a note on her chart. "You're right about the flu going around. Every other patient I've seen this week has had it."

She smiles, crosses her legs again.

He wraps the blood pressure band around her arm. She says, "Does having the flu make your heart beat faster?"

The doctor positions his stethoscope on the inside of her elbow. "It can." He pulls the stethoscope from his ears. He shines a light into one eye, then the other. "No concussion, that's a good thing." He takes her arm and rotates it. Then the other. "Hurt?"

She shakes her head.

He says, "You're going to have some nasty bruising, but nothing is broken. You need to limit your exercise until you're thoroughly over the flu virus." He jots a note on a pad of paper. "I'm excusing you from gym class."

She takes the note from him and moves to get off the table.

He pauses with his hand on the doorknob. "How is your appetite?"

"Good. Totally back to normal."

"And your periods, are they regular?"

Kas blinks. What did she say the last time? "Yes."

"Have you missed a period?"

"No, of course not. I'm not even having sex."

He nods. "Missing a period can indicate serious illness, not only pregnancy." He opens the door. "Get some extra rest. That will help you beat this flu bug."

"Dad! This was a normal, everyday gym class accident. You're making too much of it. They would have phoned you if it was serious." Kas plunks down on her bed. She hears a click on the line.

"Are you hurt? Is anything broken?"

Kas sighs. "Hi, Mom. No, I'm fine."

"Why didn't you call us when it happened?"

"I tried, I really did. Halfway through the fall, I yanked my phone from my gym pants and punched your speed dial, but my cell doesn't work inside the school. They must have the building screened so no one can do drug deals."

Now her dad speaks. "That isn't even a little funny."

"I phoned you as soon as I got home."

Her mother. "I can't believe the school didn't call. Do they have my work number?"

"And your cell numbers. And nineteen emergency contact numbers."

"You'd better come home."

No. Not home.

"Mom!"

"Just for a few days. Just until you're better. Dad and I will drive up and get you."

"Mom, no. I can't be away right now. I'll get too far behind."

"For the weekend, then."

"Tell you what. I'll call you before the weekend. If I'm not feeling way better by then, you can come up."

"But—"

"I miss you, Mom. I know you miss me. I just can't run home every time some little thing goes wrong."

"Your mother doesn't think this is a little thing, Kas."

"Okay. It's not. But it's not a big thing either. And you have to trust me to know the difference."

Her mother is crying now, and Kas wants to cry but she knows better. "Tell Tay and Liv I love them. Tell them to stay out of my stuff.... I'm kidding. Love you both."

And she disconnects.

Chapter Twenty-five

Kas finds Bal at the sinks, cleaning an immense stainless-steel soup pot. The lunch crowd has cleared out of the cafeteria, and just a few students with study periods dot the tables. She taps Bal on the shoulder, and he jumps.

"Hey." He recovers, laughs. "Why aren't you in class?"

"I'm excused." She glances into the gray dishwater. Bits of carrot and onion float in the water. She looks away. "You must be a permanent fixture at the cafeteria. I see you every time I come in."

Bal dries his forehead with his wrist. "I'm finishing up my thirty hours of community service."

"You're doing time?"

"Ha, ha. You'll do them too in grade twelve. It's supposed to round us out as human beings."

"Do you have to earn the hours only in last year?"

He shrugs. "I don't think they care when you do them."

She looks around the cafeteria hall at the overflowing garbage bins and the tables still scattered with lunchtime debris. "Looks like you could use some help."

"You offering?"

"I might be. I can only work in this period, though. And just while I'm sprung from Wellness."

He looks at her for a moment. "It's not nice work. Everyone thinks I'm nuts for volunteering here."

"So, why do you?"

Bal lowers his eyes. "I'm thinking of becoming a chef."

"That's my dream job."

"Really?"

"Oh, yeah. It's like expressing art with food. I'd be a pastry chef." She grabs a towel from beside the sink and takes the pot from him to dry. "The way butter and flour combine to form papery layers." She sighs. "And cream, whipped into glistening peaks, then heaped between the layers."

Bal laughs. "You don't look like you've ever eaten a pastry."

She sets the pot on a shelf under the counter. "I take out cookbooks from the library. I'm obsessed."

"Well, cleaning the caf is a long way from being a pastry chef."

"I'll consider it boot camp."

He dunks another greasy pot into the dishwater, removes his rubber gloves, and hands them to Kas. "You're on."

Chapter Twenty-six

Kas sets up a cardboard box for the pup near an outlet so she can plug in a heating pad. She lines the box with newspapers and scraps of old towel. The pup is splayed out next to the tangle of its litter mates, asleep. Kas strokes the pup's forehead with the tip of her finger.

"Hey, little girl. I'm right here." The pup barely stirs.

Kas opens her pack and pulls out her sketchpad and pencil. She sets up the bowl she took from the Greenes' kitchen counter and arranges the fruit. "Apples, bananas, and a bowl." She sets the bananas into the bowl. "And a pup." She gathers the sleeping pup in her hands and carefully sets it into the cardboard box next to the bowl.

"Now, a light source." She twists open the blinds on the shelter window and afternoon sunlight filters over the pup's box in pale stripes.

"It looks as if you're in jail, little girl." She sits on the floor next to the box. She makes a few adjustments in the apples, and then sketches the arrangement.

She turns when she hears the door open. Jacob, dressed in his work uniform, kneels down beside her. He studies her sketchbook.

"Amazing artwork."

"It's not." She covers her sketchbook with her hands.

"It is." He peers into the cardboard box at the pup. "She looks so small now, compared to the others. Did she eat?"

"She's due for another bottle."

"You want some help? I can mix up the stuff."

"Okay."

He gets up, and as she works she hears him running the water over the bottle. He says, "You don't want to get too attached to this pup."

"Don't say it."

"I have to. You know her chances are slim."

Kas swallows down on the catch in her throat. She looks down and blinks very fast. Maybe the tears will absorb back into her eyes, or at least drop where he can't see them.

"Kas?"

She won't look at him.

"I'm really sorry, but the shelter workers have seen this before. And it hurts worse to lose something when you love it."

Don't love. Don't love. Don't love him.

She looks at him. His eyes are tear-filled too. "I have to try."

He nods. "Okay, we'll try. I just don't want you to get hurt."

Don't feel and you won't hurt.

Chapter Twenty-seven

"The human body is amazing, what it can put up with. I mean, they basically killed him to cure him." Marin is sitting at a cafeteria table talking to Jacob. When she sees Kas, she shifts over on the bench so that Kas can slide in beside Jacob.

Jacob slips her hand into his. She leans in to him, feels his exhaled breath on her cheek. "Who are they killing?"

Marin says, "Adam Russell, the guy who left at Christmas. But he's not dying, at least not now. His brother was a match for a bone marrow transplant."

Kas feels her stomach drop. Adam Russell. His work is all over the school. He left. She started.

"Is he coming back?"

Jacob looks at her. "He can't. Not yet, anyway. He's home-schooling."

"Home-schooling." Marin shakes her head. "Poor bastard."

Jacob continues, "You should see him on the web cam. He's totally bald from the chemo, and he must have dropped to about ninety pounds. He looks like a prisoner of war."

Kas pictures Adam's shoulder blades, his ribs, the delicate bones of his spine. She thinks of the young man in the coffee shop. But it couldn't have been him. She says, "Adam is a very good artist."

Jacob nods. "When I e-mail him, I'll tell him you said so."

Now Kas drops her eyes. "He probably knows. But tell him. Just in case he's having any doubts. And tell him if he wants to come back, I'll leave."

Marin says, "Leave Whitchurch? No way. No one leaves Whitchurch, not of their own free will. The only way anyone leaves Whitchurch is if they get thrown out, or on a stretcher, like Adam. You're not going anywhere, girl."

The cafeteria is all but deserted now that classes have started. Bal is working at the sink. Kas is wiping down the tray rails. At a basket of apples, she pauses. She could have an apple. She turns the basket, inspecting the apples.

What makes you think you should get the best apple?

Kas grabs the tray rail, her head suddenly light. No apple. Her belly rumbles. She doesn't need it anyway.

Kas works her way to the end of the cafeteria counter. She rinses her cleaning cloth, then heads out to wipe tables. First, she gathers the trash people have left: crumpled lunch bags, cafeteria cartons. Someone abandoned a gravy carton, and the gravy has congealed to a wiggly gray mass. Kas scoops this into the trash barrel. Her stomach rumbles again. She clears the next table and the next. The trash barrel is almost overflowing. In the heaps of garbage, Kas spots an apple core. She glances up. Bal has his back to her. The tables near her are empty. She looks at the apple core. It's resting against a half-eaten sandwich. With another glance around her, Kas leans down and snags the apple core. She slips it into her apron pocket and heads to the washroom.

Checking that the cubicle door is latched, she brings out the apple core from her pocket. It's brown, almost entirely eaten, a big, mealy Delicious. She can see the teeth marks of its original owner. She lifts it to her mouth. It smells like discarded paper and greasy cafeteria food—like garbage. Without blinking she bites the end of the core, chews, swallows. Another bite. This time she gets seeds. She recoils from the bitter snap of the seeds and the cellulose seed packets that scrape her mouth, but she swallows. She plucks off the stem, then finishes the core. The stem, she chews for a long time.

Garbage isn't food. Garbage doesn't count.

Chapter Twenty-eight

"We could call this the last supper." Marin closes the menu and sits back against the booth cushions. "This is the only real food I'll eat before the audition. Tomorrow my mother is putting me on a cleansing regime of tofu, oats, and bean sprouts. No wheat. No dairy. No chocolate." She sighs. "I'm glad I wore my loose jeans. I'm having dessert. In fact, I might have dessert for dinner."

Kas tosses her menu down on the table. "They have angel food cake. That's what I want. You want to split one?"

"I was thinking of chocolate cake."

"Your mom will smell it on your breath." Kas glances around the tiny restaurant, the only one on Main Street. There are a few more on the highway, but Marin didn't feel like walking all the way out there. The table next to theirs is just being served—enormous platters of burgers, fries, and tall milkshakes. Kas's belly rumbles.

She pulls her eyes back to Marin, who has taken a roll from the breadbasket and is spreading it thickly with butter. Marin bites into the roll and moans, "White flour. And butter."

Kas peers into the breadbasket and selects the smallest roll, at least one hundred calories—totally forbidden. She takes the roll, and a light dusting of flour clings to her fingers. She'll eat the roll and only a bite of her dessert. Kas pushes the basket away before she can even consider the butter. Kas peels the crust from the roll, breaking it into tiny bites. Each of these she places on her tongue, then she chews each miniscule bite. Marin takes another roll.

"My mother is thrilled you're staying the night. She's making us a big supper."

Kas stops in mid-chew. "You didn't tell her we were going out for supper?"

Marin rolls her eyes. "With my mother, it's easier to ask forgiveness than permission."

The roll tastes unpleasantly sweet, as if she needs to brush her teeth. "So, will we have to eat at your house too?"

Marin waves her hand. "Just go through the motions."

Kas swallows. "I think I'll pass on the cake."

Kas leans over and speaks quietly to Marin. "Is that an apron your mother is wearing?"

Marin rolls her eyes. "She wears it when she makes spaghetti sauce."

Spaghetti.

Kas smells garlic cooking in oil. Her mouth waters. Across from her, Marin's dad flips through a stack of mail.

He tosses the envelopes on the counter behind him and turns to the girls.

"I'm starving. How about you?"

Marin's mother sets an enormous salad bowl on the table. "Help yourself, Kas."

Kas serves herself a small mound in the middle of her plate, then passes the bowl to Marin. Kas pours a small drop of dressing at the side of her plate. She dips her fork into the dressing, then stabs the salad. Just lettuce, mostly, and shredded carrots. She takes another bite.

Mrs. Jennett joins them at the table with a steaming bowl of pasta. "It's pesto. I hope you like it."

Kas watches Marin as she takes a small serving.

Not one bite of that pasta. It's coated with oil.

"Um, Mrs. Jennett, I have to pass on the spaghetti."

Marin's mother's eyes widen.

"It's just that I'm allergic to pine nuts. I'm really sorry."

Mrs. Jennett leaps up, snatching the bowl from the table just as Marin's father sets it down. "Oh, my. I'm so sorry. I had no idea. I should have asked. Are you okay? Can you breathe?"

"I'm fine. It's not that kind of allergy. I just break out."

"Oh." Visibly relieved, Marin's mother takes her seat. "Why don't I make you some plain pasta? With tomato sauce?"

"Honestly, Mrs. Jennett, the salad is delicious, and I

see you have some garlic toast. That will be tons. Really."

Marin grins at her from behind her napkin.

Mrs. Jennett eyes the pasta bowl. "I made enough for an army. I always think we'll eat more than we do."

Mr. Jennett reaches for the bowl, but she moves it out of his reach. "With the exception of you, Mr. Porkchop."

Marin's dad pats his belly. "I resemble that remark."

Kas thinks of her dad—how he used to call her Nemo because she liked to swim. Then she told him that Nemo was fat, and he never called her that again.

"My friend Jacob, he boards at the Greenes' too—he'd love this pasta."

Mrs. Jennett smiles. "I'll send it with you."

Kas is clearing the table, Marin is washing the spaghetti pot, when the phone rings. Marin dries her hands on the tea towel, then grabs the phone.

"Hi, Shay." She mouths to Kas, *About the audition.* She listens, then says, "I have to grab my calendar. Just hold on."

She puts her hand over the phone and says, "Don't worry about the kitchen. I'll clean it up when I get off the phone."

Kas waves her hands. "I'll do it."

Marin leaves with the phone.

Mrs. Jennett has put the pasta for Jacob into a large plastic tub. There's enough for two meals, even by Jacob's standards. Kas checks the lid on the container. Closed tight.

Don't even think about it.

She pries up the edge of the lid, and immediately the aroma of the still-warm pasta fills her nose.

Put it back. Now.

Kas cranes her head around the doorway. Marin's mother and father are sitting in the family room watching television. Marin has gone upstairs with the phone. The display on the charging unit for the phone says that the line is in use. Kas takes a fork from the drawer.

Just a taste.

Don't do it.

The pasta glides over her tongue in an assault of garlic and salt and herbs and oil.

Weak. You are too weak.

The hunger is stronger than she is. It coils in her jaws like a tiger, making her bite down, again, and again—growing in strength with each bite, as if the tiger is consuming her. She shovels the pasta into her mouth, watching the door, the phone—chewing and swallowing and loading her mouth. Filling her mouth. Filling herself. Tears squirt from her eyes, and her nose is running. She can barely breathe around the mouthfuls—mouthful after enormous mouthful. She eats until her jaws ache and her stomach distends. She eats until the container is empty.

Fat, weak pig. You will pay.

Chapter Twenty-nine

"It was so gross." Marin opens a ziplock bag of celery sticks and offers one to Kas.

Around them, the cafeteria is awash with lunchtime noise. Kas takes a celery stick, nicks off the end, and chews it slowly. Marin continues, "The plumber said our pipes are so old that it doesn't take much to plug them. My mom spent all day Sunday disinfecting the floor." She shudders. "It even crept into my room."

Kas keeps her eyes on the stick of celery. "My sister flushed a washcloth once and we had to call a plumber."

"It wasn't a washcloth."

Kas glances at Marin, who is looking straight ahead. Her forehead is creased. *Don't say it. Please.*

Marin says, "Plumber said it was food." She bites her celery, chews. "He said it looked like spaghetti."

Kas puts her hands against her temples. "God."

Marin turns to her, the creases in her forehead deepening. "What?"

Can she really not know? Kas threads her fingers into her hair and pulls.

"I am so sorry." She pulls until it hurts. "When I was

cleaning up the kitchen at your place—remember, your mom put spaghetti in a tub for me to take to Jacob?"

Marin shifts on the bench, so she's facing Kas. "Yes."

"When I grabbed it to put it in the fridge, the top came off, and it spilled on the floor. It all spilled on the floor."

Marin watches her, her eyes tracking her entire face.

"I felt so bad. It was such a waste, and your mom had gone to so much work to make it. I didn't want her to see it in the garbage, so I flushed it."

Marin nods. "Oh."

"I flushed it all down. That's what plugged your pipes."

Marin turns on the bench, so that she's no longer facing Kas. "Yeah…that's what my dad figured happened. He said we probably didn't run the garbage disposal when we rinsed the plates."

Kas says, "He must have been so mad."

Marin shrugs. "Don't worry about it." She turns to Kas and smiles. "They really like you, my parents."

Only losers puke. Losers with no self-control.

Chapter Thirty

Bad, so bad. He didn't want you before, and now he'll never want you.

Kas huddles outside Jacob's door, her hoody pulled over her pajama-clad knees, her hands jammed up her sleeves. She grips her arms with her fingernails, pushing hard, wishing she could open the flesh of her arms and claw it away from her bones.

So very, very bad.

If only she could turn back the clock—relive the last few hours—change what she did.

She doesn't know why she did it. She told herself that she couldn't sleep, that she needed a walk, but she took the train into the city. She knew that Whitchurch was too small, that there were no secrets in Whitchurch.

She didn't do it to hurt Jacob; that much she knows. Remorse bites at her stomach.

She's hungry, always so friggin' hungry, as if it won't go away. She went to the city to eat, but she knows better than to eat. She knows what happens when she eats, when what she wants with every ounce of her being is food.

So weak.

She met the guy on the station platform—a greasy kid a few years older, with bad skin—hanging out with a greasy clot of guys and girls. He spotted her as she got off the train; the kind of guy you turn from—run from, even. But she didn't. She stood a moment too long, looking at him. And that's all it took. He snaked his arm around her and set a joint between her fingers.

At the door, Kas listens. Jacob is dreaming; she can hear him stirring in his bed.

She doesn't know the guy's name. She told him hers because he asked. She wishes he didn't know her name, not that she'll see him again. God, she'll die if she sees him again. He asked if she was from around there, then laughed because he knew she wasn't. He didn't ask why she was there. It was as if he knew.

He couldn't know that what she wanted was to eat, and not stop eating.

Jacob's breathing is fast. He's making little moans, as if he's frightened.

The guy led her to a car in the parking lot, said they could talk there, just talk. When he kissed her, she tasted cigarette and hamburger, and it made her sick. Then he wanted her to take off her clothes, and she wanted to leave. She put her hand on the door handle to leave, but he took her hand and held it, saying that she didn't want to leave. The guy kept his clothes on.

Jacob is saying something; she can't understand what.

Afterward, the guy gave her a packet of meth, tossing it on her belly like coins. In a filthy stall in a station washroom, she flushed the drug—wanting to use it, or even more, wanting to sell it so she could eat. But it was his, and she just wanted to get rid of it.

When she got home, she stood under a trickle of shower, afraid to run the water in case anyone woke up, but she stood there until the water ran cold. Still, she wasn't rid of him.

Jacob cries out in his sleep. Kas gets to her feet, puts her hand on his doorknob. She opens his door.

His room is dark, but the streetlight outside his window sifts through the blind. Jacob is sitting straight up in bed, the sheets twisted around him. His bare chest is heaving, and his eyes are wide and unseeing. Kas creeps to the bed and puts her hand on his arm.

"It's okay. Wake up, Jacob. It's just a dream."

He turns to her, looks at her a long time, then seems to focus. "Kas?" He shakes his head, then looks down at the bedding, tugging it over himself.

"I'm sorry. Did I wake you? You were dreaming."

He shivers. He looks at the clock. "Almost five. I'm really sorry, Kas. Try to go back to sleep."

"Tell me your dream."

He looks at her.

She sits down on the edge of his bed. "Tell me."

He lies back on his pillow. "This is so weird. I was

dreaming about you. Something was after you, and I couldn't get to you to help you."

She sets her hand on his chest. "Your heart is racing."

He draws her down on the bed next to him, spooning his chest against her back. She pulls his arms tightly around her and holds his hands under her chin.

"I'm right here, Jacob. Go to sleep."

His voice is barely audible. "I love you, Kas." And he sleeps.

Chapter Thirty-one

Kas pushes her cart down the narrow aisles of the Whitchurch Foods store. She's made a list, but she doesn't need it. She knows too well what she needs to replace. A box of saltines. The Greenes buy the Costco kind, but there's no way she can get to Costco. She'll buy what she can here and refill the Costco box.

So stupid.

Graham crackers. A Costco box of Apple Cheerios. She'll have to buy two regular-sized boxes to refill it. Milk. She puts a carton of Diet Pepsi into the cart—she'll keep it in her room. A bag of chips because she craves salt. Just for the salt. She glances at the clock on the store wall. She has to get back, has to clean up. She takes her cart to the cashier, tapping her foot while the girl pushes her groceries through the scanner. Hurry. She jams the stuff into plastic bags while the girl takes her bank card. Kas keys in her pin, holds her breath. Approved. Breathes. She makes a mental note to thank her father for keeping her account topped up.

"Would you like a hand out to your car?" The girl has a chipped front tooth.

"No." Kas grabs the bag handles, amazed that they weigh so much, thinks for a minute about leaving behind the Pepsi. But, no, Diet Pepsi is something she can have. "Thanks," she adds.

The girl is watching her, spinning her earring. Her skin isn't the greatest, either. "You're new here, aren't you?" she says.

Kas pastes on a smile. "Gosh, look at the time. Gotta run." She hoists the bags and lumbers out of the store.

Too far. Too much. Bend the arms, then it's like a biceps curl. Harden the abs; make them do the work. They ache. From someone's front porch, a cat sits and watches her. No one drives by. No one is on the sidewalk. Beside the sidewalk, the grass is brown, still dead from winter. A narrow flower bed runs along the lawn and something green has sprouted—bulbs maybe. She'll just set the bags down for a minute, just rest, catch her breath. Kas rubs her wrists, raw from the plastic bags.

Stupid.

What if the Greenes find out? What if they say something to her? Or call her parents?

She craves salt. Salt. Kas rifles the bags of groceries, spots the chips. The cat on the porch is washing its face, licking its paw, then wrapping its paw around its ear. Kas reaches down and pulls out the chips. The cat is licking its butt now. Nice. She rips open the chips. She crams chips into her mouth, barely chews, grabs another handful, swallows. Grease coats her fingers, her throat. What flavor are these? She looks at the bag. Smokey Bacon. Who knew?

You are what you eat. Oink.

She tips the bag to get the crumbs, shaking them into her mouth, and feels chip crumbs rain down her neck.

Full. Too full. Kas gathers the grocery bags, grunts as she lifts them. The cat is gone, and she feels strangely alone. Her arms breathe fire. She tips her head over the flower bed, and she throws up the chips, then she kicks dirt over the mess on the ground.

Chapter Thirty-two

Marin flips through the dresses on the rack, pausing to pull out a dress and hold it up against her.

"It has to be very thin fabric. Silk is best but it costs a fortune, even at this store."

Kas stands at the next rack over. "How's this?" She holds up a sliver of a dress in a deep purple. "It's your size. I don't know about the color. It reminds me of eggplant."

Marin scampers over and grabs the dress. In a mirror on the pillar, she holds the dress up to her neck and nods with approval. "We eat eggplant. We wear *aubergine*."

She hands the dress to Kas and says, "Hold on to this one. I'll try it."

Kas folds the dress over her arm. "How do you know about this store?"

Marin continues her quest through the rack of dresses. "When we lived here in the city, my mom and I shopped at this store all the time. They have great deals on shoes too."

"I don't think I've ever bought a dress."

Marin's eyebrows shoot up. "Never?"

"What do I need a dress for?"

"Girl, I guarantee you, if you show up at Jacob's door in a dress, he'll lose his mind."

"He should lose me."

"He's crazy about you."

"Then he's crazy."

Marin comes to the end of the rack.

"Kas, you have a strange take on reality." She leads Kas by the arm to the rack of dresses. "Let's find you something."

She flips through the hangers, pulls out a dress, wrinkles her nose, replaces it on the rack. "You want a color with a shot of green to set off your eyes." She selects another dress, holds it up against Kas. "Something with a bit of flirt, to lighten you up."

"I'll never wear it, Marin."

"Sure you will. You'll wear it tonight. There's a club I know. It's kind of scummy, but they don't check ID. We'll buy you some shoes, maybe a new handbag."

"I don't have money for all this!"

Marin puts her fingers to her lips. "Shhh. We'll put it on Mommy's credit card."

"I'm not going to buy stuff with your mother's money!"

"Fine. I'll buy the dress. You can borrow it."

"Oh, and your mother won't find it strange you've bought a dress several sizes too big?"

Marin's eyebrows shoot up. "You're kidding, right?"

Kas sighs.

Marin tugs her toward the change rooms.

Marin pushes the carton of fries toward Kas. "You sure you don't want to get something?"

Kas waves away the fries. She fishes in her bag and extracts a cheese sandwich. "I brought lunch."

"You brought lunch. On a shopping trip to the city, you brought lunch. That's weird, Kas." Marin eyes the sandwich. "And that's weird bread. It's sliced so thin."

"Low calorie. You can eat twice as much."

Worthless fat thing. You don't need half of what you cram in.

Kas opens the bag and takes half a sandwich. "Want to try it? It's nonfat cheese."

Marin takes the sandwich, bites it. "Not bad, if you like Styrofoam."

Kas takes the other half, pulls out the cheese and eats it, sets the bread down on the table.

"Wait until Jacob sees you in this dress." Marin pats the store bag beside her on the table. "He won't be able to keep his hands off you. Mine looks great on you too. You can borrow it anytime."

She tosses the remaining fries onto the tray and wipes her fingers with a napkin. "You really need to buy some new clothes, Kas. Those jeans you're wearing bag at the ass."

"I will. I want to finish my diet first."

"You must be close."

Kas shakes her head. "Not yet."

Marin gets up from the table. "I'm going to get an ice cream. You want something?"

Kas pushes a bill toward her. "Get me a nonfat frozen yogurt. You want me to go with you?"

"No, you stay here and keep our spot." Marin takes the money.

"Okay, but make sure it's nonfat, not low-fat. Sometimes the worker screws it up."

Marin nods.

"And if they have the sugar-free, fat-free peanut butter flavor, get me that."

"How can peanut butter be fat-free?"

"Some things you don't want to know."

Chapter Thirty-three

Kas recognizes the club. She's been on this street before, just one block over from the train station. And inside looks just like outside—a dump.

Just your kind of place.

Marin is changing in the washroom cubicle. As if she can read Kas's mind, Marin says, "This club is so trashy, but the drinks are cheap, and they'll sell to anyone." Marin flips her jeans over the door. "And the music is good."

Kas thinks of Jacob. Is he home yet? What is he listening to?

If Jacob knew about you, he'd be disgusted.

Kas inspects herself in the mirror. The dress Marin bought for her feels snug, and she sucks in her stomach. She digs out her makeup bag and tries to fix her face.

Marin emerges from the cubicle in the purple dress. The deep color of the dress makes her hair look blue-black.

Kas nods. "That is a great dress on you."

Marin smiles. In the mirror, she tosses her hair. "Thanks. And you look amazing." She straightens the tiny strap on Kas's shoulder. Marin lights a cigarette, inhales, then sets it down on the edge of the sink. "These shoes are already killing my feet."

Kas leans closer to the mirror. "I can't walk in mine. The heels feel as if they're six feet high."

"Heels make your legs look longer. They're a necessary evil."

They pick seats at the bar and order vodka straight up. Kas sucks on a wedge of lime. Marin shifts on her stool so that she can watch the dance floor. She crosses her legs. She nudges Kas and says, "Yum."

Kas looks over her shoulder to see a man approach. He's fairly good-looking for an old guy, but he wears the same kind of jacket that her dad owns.

Kas says, "He looks like the principal from my last school."

Marin leans forward on the stool and sets her shoulder so that the lights from the bar cling to her collarbone. She says, "I'm assuming that, since you're with Jacob, he's all mine."

The man is looking at Marin. As he walks, he smooths the front of his jacket.

"All yours."

"Not that you shouldn't have some fun too. Your secrets are safe with me." She speaks to Kas without taking her eyes from the approaching man.

In the mirror over the bar, Kas watches the guy take the spot on the other side of Marin. He leans against the bar.

Marin lights a cigarette.

Kas says, "I have to use the washroom."

Her heels teeter on the grimy tile floor while she waits for the cubicle. The smell of piss and perfume and cigarette smoke makes Kas's head reel. *Hurry.* Finally, she's alone behind the plywood door, and she snaps the latch closed.

Too many calories. Too full.

Oink, oink.

There's no paper, and she rummages in her bag for a tissue. She uses the tissue to lift the seat. The underside of the seat is splattered with soil. Outside the cubicle, women laugh and talk. The music from the club blares each time someone opens the washroom door.

Kas breathes the smell of moldy floor tile, of layers of filth around the toilet, of gouged walls, and of the empty Never-Out roll. When the door opens again and the music blares, she leaves everything in the toilet. When she reaches the orange cheese slice, she knows she's done.

The guy has bought them both a drink. Kas drains hers, willing her hands to not shake the glass. He buys them both another. The music thumps, and her heels feel like nails driving into her feet. Marin is laughing at something the old guy said. Kas can't hear the guy. He's leaning against Marin, speaking into her ear.

Marin says, "We're going to dance. Come with us."

Kas blinks at the seething dance floor and shakes her head. "I can't dance in these shoes. You go."

With a shrug, Marin heads out onto the floor.

Kas finishes her drink and pulls Marin's in front of her. Marin is in tight with the guy, her dress moving under his hands. Kas turns away from the dance floor.

Hungry. Too hungry. She reaches behind the bar for another lime wedge. The bartender scowls at her but doesn't stop her. She sets the lime on her teeth, piercing each capsule of juice so that tiny trickles of sourness track down her throat.

Food. No calories. *Good.*

She peels the fruit from the rind, chewing it in small bits, then peels the white pulp and chews this. She's thinking about eating the green peel when she feels someone standing next to her.

"Hey, Kas."

Lime collides with vodka in her empty stomach.

He puts his hand on her bare shoulder. "Back so soon?"

She turns to him then; he's even uglier than he was that night in the car. Behind him, his friends are watching, snickering. She knocks his hand from her shoulder and looks away. "Piss off."

The guy takes Marin's seat.

"That's a nice dress." He runs his finger down her arm.

She yanks her arm from under his touch.

He reaches into his pocket and pulls out a pack of pills. "Want some?"

She takes a deep breath. "Look, I'm with somebody."

"I know who you're with, and she's nice." He turns to watch Marin on the dance floor. "Really nice."

Black dots float in front of Kas, and she blinks her eyes. Marin is watching her from the dance floor.

She sees him. She sees him, you idiot.

Marin says something to the old guy, who shrugs and keeps on dancing as he moves aside to let her pass.

She's coming back.

"Please. Just leave."

"Looks like she's losing the suit. Maybe you two girls want to party with us."

Make him go away.

The lime skin on the bar in front of her curls like a sneer. Kas flicks it onto the floor.

Marin arrives back at the bar and looks from Kas to the guy standing next to her, and then to the pack of pills in his hand. "Are you okay?"

The guy says, "Kas, aren't you going to introduce us?"

The black dots are deepening, stretching into black streams in front of her eyes. Marin is watching her, her face questioning.

"I don't know who you are."

Stupid. Stupid. He just called you by name.

The guy laughs. He slips his finger under the strap of

her dress and tugs it off her shoulder. "I know you."

He leans toward her as if he's going to kiss her, and she smells him and the car—the rank smell of him—and she recoils.

He says, "You know me too."

The man who Marin was dancing with appears beside her. He looks at Marin, at Kas, at the guy. "Are you ladies being bothered?"

"Ladies, my ass. Whores, more like."

Marin gasps. She grabs their things from the floor in front of the bar and takes Kas by the arm, hard. Kas stumbles off the stool. Marin curses. She bends down and yanks the heels off Kas's feet.

"Come on." She hauls Kas through the crowded club and shoves her out onto the street.

Black water rushes in Kas's ears.

Marin's mouth is a thin, hard line. She throws Kas her coat.

"Put your jeans on over the dress." They change right there on the street, the night air making them both shiver, the pavement biting into Kas's bare feet. She jams her feet into her shoes.

"Tell me you did not sleep with that creep."

Kas looks at Marin, at the disgust written on her face. She thinks of Jacob—how on some level, he must know too. She shrugs. "Like you're so pure white."

"God, Kas. He turned my stomach."

"What about that old man you were dancing with? You'd take him home to meet your parents?"

"Oh, Kas. I thought you and Jacob—"

"So what? You sound as if you care more about him than me. You probably do. You probably care a lot more for Jacob than you'd like me to know."

On the train ride home, Marin closes her eyes. Kas looks out the window at her own night-shaded face.

Chapter Thirty-four

Jacob arrives just as Kas is tucking the pup next to its litter mates. He leans over Kas and kisses her on the cheek. He's just come in from outside, and his skin feels cool. His hair is damp. Must be raining.

He says, "Marin got the part."

She keeps her eyes down. "I knew she would."

He lifts her chin. "You don't sound very happy."

She plants a smile on her face. "She's a brilliant actor."

"And crazed. She was so stressed before the audition that she barely made sense."

Kas swivels to face him. "You were talking to Marin?"

He reaches into the box and strokes a sleeping pup. "Did you two go into the city the other night?"

She takes a breath that refuses to enter her lungs. "We went shopping."

"You went to a club. She was going on and on about it."

"We went shopping, Jacob. That's all."

"No, she was saying something about going to this club and meeting some guy."

"Are you saying I'm lying?"

"No." He steps back, confused. "Jeez."

"Because if you think I'm lying, then think whatever you want." Kas crosses her arms.

"Kas, I don't think you're lying."

"Why do you keep bringing up the club? What did Marin say about the guy, anyway? What did she say about me and the guy?"

Jacob stares at her, his face working on what she said. "You and the guy?"

"He was nothing, Jacob. A slimeball."

Jacob has gone sheet white. "What do you mean? What did you do with him?"

Marin didn't tell him, you idiot.

Her stomach knots and she tastes bile.

"I said he was nothing."

His hands fall straight to his sides. His eyes go to the ceiling, as if he's tracking back time. "We have something, Kas. Why would you do that?"

You are destroying him.

She tries to swallow the acid, wishes she could hurl it. She covers her face with her hands.

You are trash. Fat white trash. Worthless. Useless. Worse than dead.

He's crying; she can tell by his voice, but she won't look at him. He says, "Did I do something to make you mad? Do you hate me? Why did you do it?"

Don't tell him. Do not tell. You've lost him anyway. Nothing you say will make you any less a slut.

"I don't know." She wants to cry, and her throat aches with it. She looks up at him and wishes she hadn't. His face is crumpled, tears streaming down his cheeks, plopping onto the floor. He swipes his eyes. She says, "I'm sorry, Jacob. I didn't mean to."

He holds up both hands. "You didn't mean to? How can you do something like that without meaning to? Were you wasted or something? Had you totally lost your mind?"

"No. Yes. Look, I said I was sorry."

He wipes his nose with the back of his hand. "You think it's enough to say sorry?"

She drops her eyes to the tiles on the floor beside her. Speckled gray tiles, speckled white tiles. Thin lines of black between each tile. Wet splotches on the tiles from their tears. She draws her finger through the tiny puddles, pulling the tears into lines across the tile.

You will drag him down until he can't get up. You will kill him.

With a shudder, her tears stop. The wet lines on the floor pebble against the wax finish.

"Kas?"

She puts her head on her knees.

"Talk to me, Kas."

She continues tracing letters on the tiles. So many tears, she could write it again and again. LOSER. LOSER. LOSER.

Everything you touch will turn to dirt.

She hears the door open, then it closes, and he's gone.

Sitting at her desk, the lamp illuminating a yellow circle on her sketchbook, Kas removes the plastic sleeve from the Exacto knife. With the palm of her left hand up, she lightly traces the whorls of her fingertips with the tip of the knife. On her index finger she finds the crescent-shaped scar from art class, and she follows the white line of the old wound, pressing harder but not so hard as to break the skin.

She imagines splotching the clean, white page with blood.

She pulls up her shirtsleeve and tracks the rivers of blue blood with the knife. Venous blood, spent of its oxygen, plodding back to the heart. With her finger she finds a pulsing artery, like a miniature heart in her wrist. She sets the tip of the knife against the artery.

You won't do it.

She pushes the knife so that a tiny bead of blood appears at the tip.

You won't do it because it's too easy.

The droplet of blood grows, quivers, then trickles onto the page.

Bleeding to death is too quick for you.

Kas draws the knife a hairsbreadth into the skin. The line springs red and blood runs down her arm.

You are an immense waste of air, a sickening lump of human flesh. You deserve to die, oh yes, but not this way. You deserve to die slowly.

Kas starts to cry, her tears falling with her blood onto the sketchbook. She drops the knife onto the desk.

Chapter Thirty-five

Mr. Randall smooths the edge of the paper. "I'm absolutely lost for words."

That must be a first. Kas flips the paper over and writes her name in one corner.

Mr. Randall turns the paper back over. He rubs his chin. "Did you pose the dog this way?"

"In a fruit bowl? No. I worked from sketches. I hope it's okay that the fruit isn't actually in the bowl."

"It looks as if the fruit has been scattered in the box, yet I can see you've composed the drawing. The overall effect is dissonant and pleasing at the same time."

"Complete…and done," she says.

If he hears her tone, he ignores it. "The charm of the pup is what first draws the eye, the way it's curled in the bowl, asleep."

He bends closer to the work. "You have minute detail in those little paws. Is it your dog?"

"Not exactly."

He shakes his head. It's as if he's talking to himself. "I don't think I've ever seen such an original still life. Look at how the bands of light echo the markings on the dog, almost emanate from the dog." He turns to her, blinking. "It's as if the dog is the source of the light."

"Well, like I said, I worked from sketches."

"Astounding."

"So, do I get a perfect mark?"

Mr. Randall flips open his roster and runs his finger down the list to Kas's name. He places a tick mark in a square. "You get completion, anyway."

Kas feels her stomach knot. "Completion?"

He answers while still gazing at the still life. "It's perfect, Kas. A flawless effort."

He closes his roster and tucks it under his arm. "One hundred percent, less fifty for the late penalty. Completion. It's a passing grade, Kas. I wish I had this on time, but I'm glad to have it at all." He turns to walk back to his desk.

Completion. Half-marks. Blood pounds in her cheeks, and her eyes burn. A crowd has gathered around her table—people murmuring their appreciation for her drawing, patting her shoulder, congratulating her.

Kas grabs the still life and stalks off to Mr. Randall's desk. She tosses the drawing in front of him and says, "The pup is all black. She doesn't have any markings. The lines you see on her coat are her ribs. She's starving herself to death." As his mouth drops open, she turns and runs from the room.

Lose it, pig. I don't care if you just ate ice cubes. I want it gone.

In the empty washroom, Kas slams the cubicle door open, and slams it again behind her, not taking the time to latch it. She has no time. She can barely breathe; she is so full. Full. She doesn't even bother to be quiet.

When she emerges from the cubicle, Stephanie is standing at the sinks looking at Kas, her eyes like dishes.

She saw. She knows.

Kas wipes her mouth with her sleeve.

Stephanie stutters and blinks. "I followed you to see if you were all right. I didn't mean to, you know, watch you." She blushes.

"It's the friggin' flu." Kas moves to a sink and turns on the water. She washes her hands, then rinses her mouth.

"No."

"Excuse me?"

Stephanie's lip begins to tremble, and she bites down on it. She says, "You put your finger down your throat. I saw you."

She looks hard at Kas, as if she's weighing her with her eyes. "I heard what you said to Mr. Randall about the pup starving herself. I think you're starving yourself."

Waves of sound crash in Kas's ears. She tries to elbow past Stephanie, but the girl blocks her path.

"I want to help you." Stephanie is blubbering now. "Please, Kas. I'm just saying it because I care about you."

"You don't care about me."

"People die from eating disorders. Their systems get totally whacked."

Kas puts her hand on Stephanie's chest. "Get out of my way." Kas pushes her against the edge of the door. "I do not have an eating disorder. At best, you are mistaken. More likely, you're jealous." Kas shoves past her. "But thanks so much for sharing your thoughts."

APRIL

Chapter Thirty-six

Outside the drugstore, Kas jumps in place, watching her reflection in the store window.

Fat. Fat. Fat.

Shouldn't have eaten. Ate at breakfast, again at lunch. Too much.

Disgusting and fat.

She pushes the door open. Hair color. Toothpaste. Toilet paper. Kas roves the aisles. Painkillers. Hair removers.

She calls to the pharmacist behind the counter. "Where are the laxatives?"

Another customer, a gray-haired woman, stops and stares.

"Not the fiber kind. I need something that works fast."

The pharmacist comes out from behind the counter. She points Kas to a display of laxatives. "Are you feeling all right?"

Kas snatches a pack of laxatives from the display. "Yes. Of course." She laughs loudly. "Oh, you thought they were for me. No, they're for my mother. She's in the worst discomfort."

The gray-haired woman clucks. "Poor dear. Was it something she ate?"

"Yeah. Like Quick-mix concrete." Kas grabs several more packages of the laxative.

The pharmacist says, "She only needs one tablet, two at the very most. Make sure she takes it with lots of water so she doesn't dehydrate."

Kas backs up to the cashier. "Hurry, please."

She pushes some crumpled bills to the cashier. The cashier counts the money out on the counter, bags the packages, and hands Kas a few cents in change.

"Keep it." Kas rips the bag out of the cashier's hand and flees the store. She pops a tablet as the door closes behind her, another before she reaches the corner. She's eating the laxatives like candy. By the time she gets to her room, sweat is beading on her forehead, and her gut feels as if she swallowed knife blades.

Chapter Thirty-seven

Lost days. How many? Three? Four? It's the flu again, she told Mrs. Greene, who stood at the bathroom door with mugs of tea, pleading, "At least drink something, Kas."

Lost days. Lost to Jacob, who watched her with hollow eyes. "I'm sorry," she said, but her voice was cracked, and she couldn't make sound. And he just shrugged. Shrugged and sighed. And she listened to him behind his closed door, and she knew he cried.

So far behind.

The steps to the school are wet with rain. She slips, and another student helps her up. Kas tries to smile, to laugh it off. She's wearing clothes from a week ago, filthy with the food she devoured and tossed. How many days? She tries to cover the worst of the stains with her hands.

The front entrance to the school seems dark, and she stumbles and catches herself. Someone has set the Vortex sculpture spinning, and the sight of it makes her stomach lurch. She follows the wall to the studio corridor, running her hand along the wall to steady herself. Must get to work. So far behind. So thirsty. Get a drink. Just a sip.

She ducks into the washroom, leaning against the

door, blinking, trying to clear her vision. Her breath is fast, but it feels as if her blood is seeping in her veins, as if she can't get enough oxygen. She lets herself slump onto the floor.

Someone wants in. They're pushing the door against her. She tells them to go away. She rests her cheek on the floor. The floor is cold, gritty against her skin.

Now there are people in the washroom, people leaning over her, taking her air. People shaking her shoulder, calling her name.

"Don't move her!" someone yells.

She struggles to sit up. A wave of black closes over her head, and she fights against it. She has to go to the bathroom. Blind, she clambers to her feet, pulling against people's legs, feeling their hands on her as she claws through the crowd, rough hands. She strikes out. Her knuckles hit the cement-block wall. Then her forehead. She feels those hands lowering her, feels hands cradling her head, feels the floor again—the cold, hard floor.

Dr. Bowen looks into one eye, then the other. His light makes her want to turn her head, but it hurts to turn her head. He looks down her throat. "When did you last eat, Kas?"

What day is it?

"Supper. I had supper last night."

"Mrs. Greene said you haven't eaten in days."

If he knows, why is he asking? "Sometimes I eat at my friend's house."

Dr. Bowen hands her a cup of apple juice. Kas takes it. She looks down at the needle taped to the back of her hand, at the long tube reaching to a clear bag hanging over her bed. "Am I in the hospital?"

He nods. "Dr. D'Angelo brought you."

The bag hanging over the bed is almost drained. "What are you putting in me?"

"Fluids. You were dehydrated." He points to the cup of juice. "Drink that."

She lifts the juice to her mouth. The apple smell is overpowering, and she lowers the cup.

"I'm feeling sick."

He grips her hand on the cup, his eyes telling her to drink it or he'll pour it down her throat. She takes a sip, and it's as if she flips a switch. The juice comes up and spews back into the cup. His eyes fly wide open. He grabs the cup from her and drops it in the sink.

"Do you think it's the flu?"

He checks her temperature. "I thought you already had it."

Too stupid.

"Maybe I didn't really get over it."

He says, "You're well enough; you can go home. Dr. D'Angelo will take you. I want you in bed, though. Call me immediately if you start feeling worse, if there's any blood in your stool or vomit, if you get dizzy again or fall."

Been there, done that. He is far too late.

He places his hand on her arm. "I want to see you in my office in a couple of days, no later, with your parents."

Acid scalds the back of her throat. "Don't call my parents."

"Dr. D'Angelo has already called them. They'll be here tomorrow."

It's as if someone is gripping her chest, squeezing her lungs so that air can't get in. "No. Please. It's the flu."

"Mrs. Greene will keep an eye on you. You need clear fluids, nothing solid until the vomiting stops."

"Let me call my parents. They know me. They'll know it's just the flu."

His voice is clipped, impatient. "I don't believe you have the flu. You can't go on like this, young lady."

Fat loser bitch. You never should have been born. Your parents will die on the highway because of you and it will be all your fault.

Chapter Thirty-eight

You put it in, pig, you can take it out. You can stop when your heart stops, when your foul carcass is worms and dirt. Then you can stop because then you'll be gone. Everything bad that happens has your name on it. You should be dead. Give it up, pig—your guts and lungs and heart. Give up your blood.

The tiled floor of the tunnel off the weight room feels cold on her bare feet. Kas strips off the rest of her clothes, shivering in the darkness, grateful for the darkness so that she doesn't have to look at herself. The breaker for the tunnel was easy to find, clearly marked on the panel in the utilities room. It would have been easy for someone to trip the breaker any time she and Marin had been down here. She shivers.

She kneels on the floor. She puts two fingers in her mouth, her knuckles scraping on her teeth, her nails clawing tracks in the back of her throat. She drives the fingers deeper, and her breath catches. Tears spring to her eyes. When nothing more comes, she lies on the floor and draws her knees to her chest.

She feels the tunnel door open as a slight change in pressure on her eardrums. She opens her eyes, thinks she's gone blind, then remembers she is in the dark. She hears a click, then a lighter flares. In the flash of small light, Kas sees that it is Marin.

"Kas, are you down here?"

Kas flattens herself against the floor.

Go away. Do not see me. I am not here.

The tunnel door thumps partially closed, as if it's stopped against something. The water bottle. Kas smells lighter fluid. She can see the small flame of the lighter and in it, Marin's wide eyes.

The cold floor drives into her hip bones, and Kas aches to move.

Don't move. Don't even breathe.

"Kas?"

If she finds you, you are dead.

The tunnel door squeaks opens.

You are such a screw-up.

Kas waits for the door to close, but it doesn't. She can see the faint glow of the red exit lights in the darkened weight room. In that lighter darkness, she sees that Marin has propped the door open wide.

Screw. Screw. Screw-up.

Lights come on in the weight room. The sudden light washes down the tunnel like water. Kas scrabbles to her feet, fleeing the rush of light.

"Kas? Kas, is that you?"

Run.

Black rushes up between her eyes.

Too fast. Got up too fast. Kas reaches blindly for the tunnel wall.

"Kas!"

She hears heels clicking on the tunnel floor, running. Her knees crash against the floor, then her forehead.

Someone is crying.

"God, Kas. Don't move."

Chapter Thirty-nine

"Don't come near me."

"Okay. I'll stay right here." Marin squats down.

In the pale light, Kas huddles with her arms wrapped around her knees. Vomit has dried into a caked mess on her hands. "You need to go away."

"Everyone is looking for you, Kas. I'm not going anywhere. Not without you."

Kas closes her eyes.

"You're shivering. Let's put your clothes on."

Kas turns her face away. "Why do you bother with me?"

"We'll clean you up a bit. I'm going to get the water bottle."

When she takes the water bottle, the door will close. When the door closes, the tunnel will be dark again, and she'll leave you alone.

Kas pushes herself to her knees.

Slowly, you idiot.

She hears Marin's footsteps retreating down the tunnel.

She's leaving you down here to rot. You are nothing to her.

Kas sees Marin in the doorway. Then the light shrinks to blackness. She reaches out for the tunnel wall. After the light, the darkness in the tunnel solidifies around her. She takes a step, and another, away from Marin.

Kas feels a hand on her arm. "Ah, Kas, there you are."

She hears the click of Marin's lighter, and her friend appears in the small circle of the flame. Marin hoists the water bottle and, with her teeth, pops open the lid. "We'll get the worst of it off. Then I'll take you to the shower."

Holding the lighter with one hand, Marin aims the water bottle so that a stream of water hits the top of Kas's head.

Kas gasps. Her hands come up to stop Marin.

"Put your hands down, Kas."

She does.

Marin holds the water bottle between her legs and uses Kas's T-shirt to dab Kas's face, removing the caked vomit. "I'm going to warm the water for you. Don't get grossed out."

Kas almost laughs at this.

Marin takes a swig from the water bottle and warms it in her cheeks. Then, in a thin stream, she spits it on Kas's forehead. Kas tips her face. Marin warms another mouthful, and then expels it on Kas's cheeks. Kas's eyes are open, and the water flows over her cheeks and jaw, down her neck into the deep creases of her collarbones.

Working quickly, Marin cleans Kas's face. She uses her

finger inside a clean bit of the T-shirt to remove the guck from Kas's ears. She wipes her neck. She warms water in her mouth as she works, doling it out.

"Let's see your hands." For these Marin squirts the water right from the bottle, sloughing off the guck. She inverts Kas's hands and douses the palms. "Your lines go deep. You were born old."

"Born dead. Like the pup."

For a moment, their eyes meet. Then Kas looks down. When she's finished, Marin tosses the T-shirt to the floor. With the last of the water, she washes her one hand, then the other.

"Now, your clothes."

Kas turns her back to Marin. Marin reaches out and traces the relief of Kas's spine. "I'm so sorry, Kas. I had no idea."

Kas sighs. Under Marin's hand, she feels her ribs come apart with every breath.

Marin says, "You drew me with ribs like this."

Marin retrieves the pile of Kas's clothing. She holds Kas's jeans so Kas can step into them. "Two of you could wear these jeans." Kas stands limp, allowing Marin to put her arms into her coat, lifting her chin so that Marin can zip it.

Kas says, "For a while, I thought you heard it too."

"Heard what?"

Kas shakes her head.

Marin draws Kas closer. "How could I not have seen what was happening to you?"

She's on to you, pig. What a loser you are. You never should have let her get so close. Now you've smeared her with your poison. You've tainted her, just like everyone else.

JUNE

Chapter Forty

In the small window in the door, Kas sees Jacob sitting with his back to her in the glassed-in booth. Another student sits next to him and makes small adjustments on a panel of sliding switches. Kas taps on the door. Jacob has headphones on and doesn't hear, but the other guy motions for her to come in. He pokes Jacob in the arm and thumbs toward the door. Jacob turns, and when he sees Kas, he yanks off the headphones and pushes back from the panel.

"Kas."

Eight weeks since she left—since her parents took her from the hospital in Whitchurch to the hospital at home. She knows it's been eight weeks because her mother crosses off the days on the calendar. Otherwise, there's no way for Kas to know. Time passes, but with no reference points for her—no meaning.

Jacob is standing, but he hasn't moved. He's looking at her as if he doesn't recognize her.

She told herself she wouldn't cry.

He crosses the booth in two long strides. "Are you back?"

Kas shakes her head. "Just for a few days—for Marin's play." Kas looks over her shoulder toward the door. "My mom is with me."

Jacob puts his hands in his pockets. He holds his shoulders tight, as if he's holding himself in check. His gaze slips to her bare arms, then his eyebrows crease and he looks away. Without looking at her, he says, "Marin's in final rehearsals today and tomorrow."

Kas nods. "I know. We're getting together later." She watches his face, but he doesn't look at her. "Anyway, I thought I'd say hello." She backs toward the door.

"Yeah." Jacob turns to the glass panel looking down at the stage. "I better get back to it."

She watches as he takes his chair. He looks pale, and when he reaches for the headphones, his hands are trembling.

"Jacob."

He pauses. She sees him breathe in, close his eyes.

She says, "I didn't have a chance to say goodbye...." She swallows. "To say anything."

His gaze is down, as if he's talking to his shoes. "Of course not. You were sick."

She is so tired that her throat aches. "Sick. Yes."

He turns in his chair so that his back is to her. He puts on the headphones, wraps his hands around his forehead like a visor, drops his head. As she pushes the door closed behind her, she sees his shoulders shaking.

Kas sets her mother's small bag on the bed—her bed from before. The Greenes couldn't rent out her room so close to the end of the school year, so it's been empty. Her father came up one weekend and packed all her stuff. The room feels familiar and strange at once. She says to her mother, "I'll take the floor."

Jacob isn't at home but the door to his bedroom is closed. In the bathroom, Kas leaves the door open so her mother doesn't freak. The bathroom smells like Jacob—his shampoo, mouthwash.

She hears footsteps bounding up the stairs and comes out of the bathroom to see Marin coming for her at a full run, her arms wide. She's wearing shorts and a tank top, and her hair is gathered on the top of her head.

"Kas, Kas, Kas!" Marin swoops her into her arms and spins her around. "I've missed you so much. You have to tell me everything."

Kas laughs. "After you tell me everything."

Marin hauls her toward the bedroom. Kas says, "Ah, Marin, my mother is with me. Let's go for a walk."

Outside, the sun feels hot on Kas's shoulders. Marin links her arm through Kas's.

"I'm so glad you're here. I bought you tickets for opening night, front row. I want a friendly face to look at. My mother is certifiable. She's on the phone to the papers as we speak, trying to get me interviews."

Marin pauses for a breath. "And there's a big party

after the dress rehearsal, and you'll have to come. I'm getting my nails done again—I can't stop chewing my thumb." She stops, looks at Kas. "I'm glad you're here."

Kas takes in the tidy green lawns of Whitchurch, the trees in full leaf, the gardens tumbling with flowers. "I thought I was happy here."

Marin is quiet, then she says, "You're still losing weight."

Kas shrugs. "They don't let me see the scale."

Marin draws her in close. "You are a beautiful person, Kas."

"I like hearing you talk. Talk, Marin. Walk with me and talk."

Chapter Forty-one

The Latcham Gallery is cool and dark—the air like water after the heated concrete of the sidewalk. The front reception desk is empty, but Kas can hear people talking. Their voices echo in the gallery. Beside the reception desk an easel holds a poster advertising the Whitchurch school show. She peeks around the partition.

Mr. Randall, in jeans and a golf shirt, is standing on a ladder hanging a picture. Kas recognizes the picture from Stephanie's sketch of the bowl of fruit. She moves closer. Mr. Randall sees her.

"Kas." He climbs down the ladder. "You made it."

Kas motions to Stephanie's still life. "She's very good."

He follows her gaze. "Stephanie did well this term. I look forward to her work next year." He clears his throat. "Will you be back in September?"

Kas looks down at her feet. "I gave up my spot."

"Maybe I could talk to Dr. D'Angelo—put a good word in for you."

Kas tries to smile. "Thanks, but there's some other stuff going on for me."

He nods. He knows. Everyone knows. He says, "Did you see where I hung your work?"

She looks at him. "You put mine in?"

He smiles. "This way." He leads her to a black-paneled display. Soft lamps cast light in careful arcs over her still life of the pup. "I framed it for you."

She nods. "I like it."

"You've had some offers on it apparently."

Her eyes move to a set of three drawings mounted near the still life. "Hey, you put in my drawing of Marin. And my sketch of her all stretched out."

She goes close to the sketch and smiles. A small note is mounted with the sketch—Not for Sale.

"It's on loan from a private collection."

"And my self-portrait." Kas touches the corner of the drawing. "That's a little too real."

Mr. Randall stands with her. "I didn't know, Kas. I don't know how I couldn't have known."

Kas shakes her head. "These are the only drawings in the show that aren't still lifes."

He looks at her and sighs. "It's life."

Chapter Forty-two

The music from the party rockets out from Marin's front door. Behind Marin, it looks as if the entire school is packed into her living room. Marin grabs Kas's hand and pulls her in.

"You look stunning."

Kas tugs on the aubergine dress. Marin's mother took the side seams in for her and stitched up the bodice so it wouldn't gape on her chest. Kas's mom took her to get her hair done, and they loaded it with product to give it some shine. She teeters on her high-heeled sandals and takes a deep breath. The music is loud, and she likes that. She scans the room.

As if Marin can read her mind, she says, "He's in the kitchen—no surprise."

She takes Kas's elbow and leads her through the crowded living room. People are dancing. Some stop as she passes and greet her. Some just stare. She spots Stephanie, who pushes her way to her and gives her a gentle hug. It's loud, and Kas can't hear what Stephanie is saying, but she nods as if she can. The dining room table is loaded with pizza boxes and cans of pop. Kas grabs a can

169

of Diet Pepsi and holds it close to her as she follows Marin to the kitchen.

Marin's mother is at the counter arranging a platter of grapes. Jacob is at the table in the middle of an enormous plate of what looks like roast chicken and mashed potatoes. Marin shoos her mother out of the kitchen, sets Kas down at the table with Jacob, and leaves them, closing the kitchen door behind her.

Jacob wipes his mouth with a napkin. He sits back from the table. He's wearing a shirt, open over a T-shirt. Kas imagines she can smell the scent of his collar, his aftershave.

"Hey, Jacob."

He leans away from her. "I wondered if you would show."

She studies his face. "Marin…she wanted me to be here."

He nods. He takes a long time looking at her face. Finally, he says, "Your hair looks nice."

She pops open the Diet Pepsi. It's not as cold as she likes it, but it has the burn she seeks. He watches her drink. He looks at her arms, at the dress. "Maybe you want something to eat?"

She feels her cheeks growing warm. "Oh, no. I'm fine."

He nods. "The chicken is good."

The meat is in shreds on his plate. In the potatoes, she sees the stripes of the tines of his fork. He pushes the plate toward her.

"I can't, Jacob."

His mouth tightens. "You can't eat chicken."

He hauls the platter of grapes to the table, shoving it in front of her. "So eat grapes."

Mrs. Jennett has laced bunches of grapes in a twine of red and green so that it created a pleasing pattern. Kas looks at Jacob. A tiny muscle in his cheek flexes. She examines the platter of grapes.

"Just take one." His voice is so sharp that she jumps. "Here." He grabs a bunch from the platter and tosses them down in front of her. "Eat them." He grabs another handful and scatters them on the table.

A small, soft grape rolls under his napkin. She reaches for it, watching him, and takes it between her fingers. The grape is too soft, too ripe. She sets it in her mouth.

He slams his hand down on the table. Grapes bounce off the table, into her lap, onto the floor. He kicks his chair back. "Why are you doing this to yourself?"

She bows her head.

He's crying. "You think you're just killing yourself?"

Tears spill off her cheeks, black tears, staining the dress. "I watched that pup grow smaller and smaller, and it just stopped eating. We couldn't make it eat, and it died."

She folds her hands in her lap.

"I thought I could stop loving you so it wouldn't hurt anymore. But I can't." He's sobbing now. She glances at him. His face is red, twisted, streaming with tears.

What would she say to him? That she can't eat? That if she eats, she eats until she's sick, and she'd rather starve? She lowers her eyes.

She hears the back door slamming open. She looks up to see him gone.

She takes the grape from her mouth. She places it in Jacob's napkin and wraps it once, twice. Then she gets up and goes to the garbage. She lifts away the potato peelings, the Styrofoam tray from the chicken. Under these, she tucks the napkin, then replaces the garbage on top of it.

If she could, she would tell him that she can't stand to look at herself. That if she could, she would carve herself away from her bones.

Chapter Forty-three

The school theater is packed. Kas takes her seat in the front row next to her mother, and opens the program.

"There she is," she says, pointing to the program. "Marin Jennett as Lady Macbeth." She sees Jacob's name too, as Sound Engineer. She looks over her shoulder at the darkened glass of the sound booth high above the theater. Can he see her?

The lights dim, and the audience grows quiet. Players move across the stage, so close to the edge that Kas can see the stitching in their costumes, their sweat beading on their made-up faces.

She would stay in this seat forever, if she could, watching unseen.

At Marin's entrance, a murmur lifts from the audience. Her gown is fine white fabric tied with gold, slim to her body and cut low in the front. Her hair is wound into a long black braid, woven with the same gold strands as the dress. Kas watches Marin breathe, the deep breath she always takes just before she speaks her part. Kas remembers the lines from practicing with Marin. She could recite them; she knows them so well.

In Act Five, when Marin falls to her knees, the audience gasps. Marin twists her hands into her dress, wringing the fine fabric until it's tight over her legs, until Kas sees the hollows between her leg muscle and bone. Marin is Lady Macbeth. She's the fractured spirit of a woman devoured.

Kas's breath catches. Her mother is weeping. She sees it too. Watching Marin is like looking in a mirror. On stage, Marin is Kas.

Chapter Forty-four

Packing boxes are open on Jacob's bed. His shelves are empty; his desk is bare. A night breeze sways the spruce trees outside his open window. The house is quiet. Kas stands at his doorway in her robe and fuzzy socks. She taps on the door.

He turns, sees her, drops his eyes. "Kas, I'm sorry."

From the doorway, she reaches out her hand, revealing the canister of ash. She says, "I took it from the shelter."

He moves to her and takes the canister, opens it. His eyes widen. He shakes a bit of ash into his palm.

"Let me." With her finger, she rubs the ash into the lines of his palm. He closes his hand around hers.

"I don't understand you."

She laces her fingers through his.

"No." He sets the canister on his desk and takes her other hand. "I do understand you. But I don't understand your sickness."

"Anorexia and bulimia."

"Both?"

"Package deal."

He brings her hand to his lips. "It's not enough that I love you, is it?"

"It helps." She pulls his arms around her. "Where are you going?"

He rests his cheek on the top of her head. "Home, for now. University. I don't really know."

"You should write music."

"Not much of a living."

"But it's what you want."

"And you?"

She breathes him in. "I want to get normal."

He pulls back so he can see her face. "Treatment?"

She nods. "Time."

He folds her against his chest. "Any good universities in your town?"

"Only music schools."

"What about art schools?"

"I think they have a cooking school."

"Well, that would be all right too." He takes her hand. "What do you want to do with the ashes?"

She sits Jacob down at his keyboard. "I want to set them free." She climbs onto his desk and sits cross-legged at the open window. She pours the ashes into her cupped hand. "Play for me."

He sets the volume on the keyboard, then begins to play.

She recognizes the tune, "It's my song."

He smiles.

She holds her hand at the window and closes her eyes. She opens her hand until the breeze weaves around her fingers. She imagines the ashes and the music floating together on the night air. When she opens her eyes, the ashes are gone.

"They're probably settling on my car."

Kas looks out into the night. "No. They're free."

Jacob gets up and circles his arms around her shoulders. "I'm sorry about the pup."

She sighs.

"Dr. Dee took the mother dog."

Kas spins to face him.

"She wanted one of the pups, of course, but I convinced her that the mother dog deserved a chance. She brings the dog to school with her."

Kas smiles. "Lucky dog."

"That's what she named her. Lucky."

"I knew that."

He runs his fingers down the angles of her cheekbones. He tips her face, holding her with hands so soft and strong that she wonders how she could love him any more than she does right now.

Chapter Forty-five

"Twenty minutes. That's my limit."

Her mother is standing on the Greenes' porch with a look on her face that means business. Over her shoulder, Kas gives her mother a thumbs-up.

"She's trusting you to turn me around," Kas says. Jacob makes elaborate stretching motions, his bare white legs ridiculous in his gray shorts and squashed Adidas.

Marin jogs in place, perfectly made up, in exactly matched running tank and shorts. She says, "Like Jacob could handle more than twenty minutes anyway."

Jacob puffs up his chest. "I'm a seasoned athlete."

To Kas, Marin rolls her eyes.

Kas takes up the position between her friends. "Make it count, guys. This run has to sustain me for three hours, listening to Mom's talk radio stations in the car."

Marin slips one arm through Kas's. Jacob takes the other. He says, "Today's the longest day of the year."

Marin says, "The shortest night."

Kas begins to jog. "A good time to start."

Author's Note

Whenever authors write about eating disorders, they risk trivializing the suffering of real victims, who live in a world that is unreadable in its horror. In writing *Zero,* I hoped to give readers a glimpse into the dark world of self-destruction that plagues people with eating disorders.

Eating disorders are complex and devastating. People with eating disorders suffer in their health, their work, their school lives, their friendships, and their family relations. Below are some facts about eating disorders and some resources for further reading. Please note: this information is general and should not replace evaluation and treatment by a qualified professional.

What are eating disorders?

There are two major types of eating disorders: Anorexia Nervosa (anorexia) and Bulimia Nervosa (bulimia). A person with anorexia severely restricts food, which leads to drastic weight loss. A person with bulimia eats without control, often large amounts of food (called *bingeing*), and then gets rid of the food (called *purging*) through vomiting and the use of laxatives, diuretics, and enemas. Binge eating is also considered an eating disorder.

What causes eating disorders?

There is no single cause for eating disorders. They may begin with preoccupations with food and weight, but eating disorders are not about food and weight. Anorexia is not about being vain, and it is not a simple plea for attention. Bulimia is not just an addiction to food. An eating disorder is a serious and complex problem—an outward sign of a deeper emotional struggle going on inside.

Aren't people with eating disorders just trying to be thin?

Western society loves thin people. Look at all the images of celebrities, models, and actors whom we admire. But there's a difference between becoming thin to satisfy society's expectations and becoming thinner and thinner in order to erase oneself from the planet.

Who develops eating disorders?

Eating disorders are more common among teenage girls and young women, but boys and young men can also develop them. Eating disorders occur in individuals of all ages, all backgrounds, all ethnic groups, all weights, and all body shapes.

How does a person develop an eating disorder?

Developing an eating disorder is not intentional. It happens gradually over time. An eating disorder might start from a diet that becomes progressively more obsessive. Eating disorders are a symptom of an inner conflict that may have ravaged a person for years.

Can a person have "a mild case" of anorexia?

All eating disorders are potentially dangerous and must be taken seriously. An eating disorder can become severe alarmingly fast, as happens with Kas.

Are eating disorders fatal?

People die from eating disorders at any body weight. Anorexia has the highest mortality rate of all mental disorders. Statistics vary. According to the South Carolina Department of Mental Health, twenty percent of people suffering from anorexia will die prematurely from complications, such as cardiac arrest, an electrolyte imbalance, and even suicide. Death can occur many years into the disorder or within months of onset.

Can eating disorders be cured?

Anorexia and bulimia are curable disorders particularly if they are identified early, treated by trained therapists, and if people with these disorders and their families get sufficient support. The earlier an eating disorder is discovered and treated, the better the chance for recovery. Treatment can be costly, and people with eating disorders often relapse. Prevention is the best course.

Can I recover on my own?

According to the National Eating Disorders Association, it is unlikely that most people will get well completely on their own. NEDA recommends professional guidance and care.

Can a person have both anorexia and bulimia?

Yes. Sometimes a person will alternate between anorexia and bulimia.

How can I tell if someone I know has an eating disorder?

Not everyone who tries to lose weight has an eating disorder. People who use drastic methods to lose weight or who are bingeing and purging are risking their health and may develop an eating disorder.

Here are the physical signs of an eating disorder:

- Noticeable weight loss
- Menstrual periods become irregular or stop
- Extreme sensitivity to cold
- Muscle weakness
- Erratic sleeping habits
- Thinning of hair; hair loss
- Yellowish tone to skin
- Swollen facial glands; sore throat; visible dental problems
- Scarring, red abrasions on hands, knuckles

Behavior and attitude signs of an eating disorder:

- Appears preoccupied with food; prepares food for others but doesn't eat it
- Checks weight several times each day
- Displays strange eating habits—cuts food into tiny pieces, for example
- Eats only diet foods
- Consumes large quantities of diet drinks
- Becomes preoccupied with what others think
- Perception of body shape is different from what it really is
- Displays an intense fear of gaining weight
- Displays guilt and fear about eating meals
- Refuses to eat in front of others

- Claims to have already eaten
- Visits the bathroom right after eating
- Withdraws socially
- Maintains rigid exercise regimes
- Uses laxatives, enemas, diet pills
- Wears baggy clothes to disguise weight loss
- Denies there is a problem

Emotional and personality signs of an eating disorder:

- Has difficulty making decisions
- Appears depressed, irritable, anxious, or moody
- Appears extremely sensitive to comments or criticism
- Displays an attitude of self-loathing
- Appears impulsive
- Appears to have poor concentration
- Appears to have impaired judgment
- Appears to be driven or obsessive

What can I do to help?

If you have a friend or family member who shows signs of an eating disorder—especially an obsession with food and body image—you can make a difference. A person with an eating disorder may deny that anything is wrong. Offer support without judging the behavior.

- Let her know she is safe with you, and that you're there to listen.

- Tell him you care about him.
- Encourage her to speak to a parent or trusted adult.
- Encourage him to see a doctor, nurse, dietician, or counselor (check the NEDA website for referrals).
- Focus on her well-being rather than her appearance.
- Avoid compliments about his looks.
- Be optimistic and have hope.
- Take care of your own health.

Additional information:

Your library will have current books and articles on eating disorders. The following websites are a good starting point to understand the complex nature of eating disorders.

> National Eating Disorders Association (NEDA):
> 603 Stewart Street, Suite 803
> Seattle WA 98101
> 1-800-931-2237
> www.edap.org

National Eating Disorder Information Centre (NEDIC).
A program of the University Health Network in Toronto,
Canada. Mandated by Ontario Ministry of Health:
> 1-866-633-4220
> www.nedic.ca

About the Author

Diane Tullson is the author of novels for teen readers,
inc_____ *Highway.*
Bo_____ literature
an_____ er of mag-
azi_____ e in Delta,
Br_____ amily and
the_____